ECHO STILL

ECHO STILL

Tim Tibbitts

Green
Bean
Books

Green
Bean
Books

First published in 2018 by Green Bean Books,
c/o Pen & Sword Books Ltd,
47 Church Street, Barnsley, S. Yorkshire, S70 2AS
www.greenbeanbooks.com

ISBN 978-1-7843-8305-3

Library of Congress Cataloging-in Publication Data available

Typeset by JCS Publishing Services Ltd, www.jcs-publishing.co.uk

for Kittie

In loving memory of my grandmother,
Patricia Miller Price, 1919–1986

"It is hard to sing of oneness when our world is not complete, when those who once brought wholeness to our life have gone … Yet no one is really alone; those who live no more echo still within our thoughts and words, and what they did is part of what we have become."

"The Blessing of Memory,"
Gates of Prayer for Shabbat and Weekdays

ONE

If there was one place in the whole world where Fig felt truly at home it was the soccer field. At the moment, the guys were doing a drill—working in groups of three, one-touch passing until they'd made seven touches. Whoever made the seventh touch fired a shot on goal. Fig was working with Tony and Raj. Tony was Fig's best friend, and the three boys had been playing soccer together since second grade.

Fig, a natural righty, was working hard today on using his left foot more. In the drill, he was in the middle between the two others, dishing the ball left and right. Tony made the fifth touch back to Fig, who stepped over the ball then nudged it backward with his left heel to Raj, who hammered it home past a tired-looking Simmy.

"Goal!" Fig shouted, pumping his fist in the air, and he and Tony fake mobbed Raj, rubbing his head and pounding on him as though he'd just won the World Cup.

Waiting for their next turn, Fig and Tony watched another trio working the ball around. When Joey D. took a shot and missed, Gus Starks barked at him.

"C'mon man! I was wide open. *Pass* the ball!"

"What's Starks talking about?" Tony asked Fig. "He doesn't even know how to pass."

Gus Starks was a ball hog. He was also a bully in general. And, starting next week, he was set to be the newest player on the Elites, the premier traveling team Fig dreamed of playing for. Made Fig want to puke.

"You know he stinks, right?" Tony said. "He scores a lot because he's a ball hog, but Starks is no better than you. You're the one who should be moving up to the Elites."

"Yeah, well, that's not happening, is it?" Fig said.

"The good news is, after Saturday's game, no more Gus," Tony said.

"Right. Good riddance."

Coach called a five-minute break and shouted for everyone to get some water. The early October afternoon was unseasonably hot—Fig could use some water—but he'd forgotten his water bottle, so as the others headed over he stayed on the field and worked on a new trick he'd seen on YouTube.

It had been a rough day. D- on a science quiz. Completely forgot an assignment in math class. And then when Rachel Friedman asked him in study hall if he would "be a sweetheart" and make a few posters for the school play, the Wicked Stepsisters—that's what Tony called Rachel's mean friends—made him feel like such a jerk. He was annoyed at himself for saying yes. She was just using him. Fig's dad and Rachel's dad worked together, and Fig and Rachel had apparently known each other since before they were born, but they weren't friends anymore. Not really. Now that they were in seventh grade, Rachel had developed a trio of stuck-up friends who barely acknowledged his existence.

It was good to be outside now. On the field.

"All right, split-squad scrimmage," Coach announced, clapping his hands to indicate the break was over. "Drag that goal closer," he instructed, pointing to where he wanted it placed. Shortening the field would reduce the running back and forth—no one's favorite part anyway—and emphasize passing and foot skills.

Behind Tony, Fig saw his dad's car. Was it time to go already? On Wednesdays Fig had to leave practice early, which he hated doing, to go to class at the synagogue, which he didn't love either. And scrimmaging was the best part of practice, the most like a real game.

"Oh, man," he said, gesturing behind Tony.

Tony turned around. "Oy vey," he said and smacked his hand against his forehead. Besides eating an occasional bagel, "Oy vey" was the only thing remotely Jewish that Tony knew. He'd picked it up from some movie, and he got the biggest kick out of saying it every time Fig's dad came to get Fig for class. A real comedian.

Fig gave Tony another smack on the forehead, then scampered away before his friend could retaliate.

Fig rode his bike to practice, so it was embarrassing that his dad came to pick him up in a car. The temple was only three miles from the practice field, and Fig could have ridden his bike there. While his father had never said it in so many words, Fig was pretty sure his dad didn't trust him to leave practice on time. He was probably right.

Fig's father got out of the car and stuck out his clenched hand for the fist bump that had replaced hugging in public when Fig was in fourth or fifth grade. "Hey, chief."

They strapped the bike onto a rack on the car.

"Good day?" his father asked when they got back in the car.

"It was all right."

"School go okay?"

Fig nodded.

"Lot of homework?"

Fig shrugged.

"Well, my day was fine. Thanks for asking," his father said with mock enthusiasm. "Great chat." He turned on the radio. It was tuned to NPR. It was always tuned to NPR. "You can put on whatever you want."

Fig nodded but did not reach up to change the station.

When Fig was born, twelve and a half years ago, his mother apparently used to joke that her son had gotten her husband's last name but her religion. Like it was some sort of deal they had made. His dad's last name, Newton, wasn't Jewish, but they made up for that by giving him the unmistakably Jewish first name of Elijah. That name stuck until second grade, when a classmate gave him the not very clever nickname of Fig—"You know, 'Fig Newton.' Like the cookie!" Now even his dad called him Fig.

His father had been raised "vaguely Protestant," as he put it, but except for a funeral and a couple of weddings, Fig had never seen his father go to church. Evidently, religion wasn't high on his list either. But he had promised Fig's mother that their son would be raised Jewish and go through the preparation for a bar mitzvah. The problem was, Fig didn't really feel Jewish. He wasn't sure what to feel where religion was concerned.

When the car came to a stop in front of the synagogue, Fig's dad turned and gave him a serious look. "Gigi's coming to stay with us for a few days."

That was random.

"Gigi?" Fig asked.

Fig's Charleston grandmother, his mother's mother, came north to visit for a week every summer. And Fig went to South Carolina to stay with her at spring break. But they never saw each other in October.

"She's going to have a few tests at Great Lakes."

Great Lakes Medical Center was the big hospital in town. As their ads constantly assured everyone, Great Lakes was "a world-class medical center," a place where famous athletes and oil-rich sheiks came for surgeries. Gigi needing to come for "a few tests" didn't sound like good news to Fig.

He was late, as always, and the halls of the synagogue were empty. At the end of a long, dim hallway, light seeped out from under a door. This end of the hallway had been strewn with a few old, overstuffed couches to create some grown-up's version of a teen atmosphere. The custodian was on his hands and knees, picking up broken pretzels from the before-class snack. Paper cups were scattered on the tables and on the arms of the sofas. Fig was tempted to grab a handful of pretzels from the bowl on the table, but he held back.

He put his face to the thin vertical window in the classroom door and looked in. Dr. Bischoff was gesticulating wildly. Dr. Bischoff was not only weird—on that Fig could see eye-to-eye with the other kids—but he was also confusing. A microbiologist at the university, Dr. Bischoff was very into being Jewish, but he had once admitted to the class that he wasn't even sure about the existence of God. That combination just didn't make sense to Fig. Shouldn't a religion teacher be sure about his beliefs?

From his vantage point, Fig could see the very large bald spot on the back of Dr. Bischoff's head. He pressed his nose harder against the glass. Two girls were not-sosecretly looking at a magazine together, and behind them Fig could see a boy, maybe his name was Jacob, nodding off like an old man in front of a TV. Fig dreaded the thought of going in. The only thing that kept him from walking right back outside was the soccer trip Fig and his father were planning for next summer. His father insisted on calling the trip—to see soccer matches in four different cities in ten days—"your bar mitzvah trip." Fig knew he was a jerk for being anything other than super grateful, but more and more these days the trip was feeling like a bribe to get Fig to go through with this bar mitzvah thing.

Dr. Bischoff's grinning face popped up on the other side of the glass. Fig jumped back, forced a smile, then opened the door.

"The Prophet Elijah, ladies and gentlemen!" Dr. Bischoff practically shouted. He was the kind of teacher who liked to make up goofy nicknames for all his students. "What a great honor," he added with a bow, then handed Fig a piece of paper with an outline for the evening's lesson. Fig felt his face grow warm as he slunk to the back of the small classroom and took a seat behind a girl with three ponytails. He would have preferred to slip in unnoticed, but the class was too small for that. The eight or nine other kids all seemed to know each other from years of Hebrew school together. Fig knew no one. Whatever. He had friends. He didn't need friends here. He looked up at the clock—eighty minutes! As Dr. Bischoff tried to engage the class in a discussion of repairing a broken world, Fig took out a pen and committed himself to a careful study of the trio of braids in front of him, a detailed sketch that stretched like tentacles around the words on the page.

REMEMBERING NINA
Interview with Greta Nussbaum

You've told me Nina was a big sports fan. Did she—

Baseball.

What?

Your mother was a big baseball fan. She didn't have much time for other sports. And for her, baseball was all about the Braves. She loved her Braves; she was pretty fierce about it, actually.

Baseball. Got it. So, how did she become such a big Braves fan?

Unlike some of the questions you've been asking, that's an easy one: her father. He enjoyed sports of all varieties, but his first love was baseball, and he was determined to turn your mother into a fan. When the Braves came to Atlanta in 1966, he vowed that he'd get her to at least one game every year. You see, we never had a major league team in the entire South before '66.

Was she really there the night Hank Aaron broke Babe Ruth's all-time home run record?

She sure was, and I was none too happy about it, either.

What? Why not? It was the opportunity of a lifetime.

Two reasons: first of all, it was the second night of Passover. I was just livid with your grandfather for even thinking about taking the girls three hundred miles to Atlanta on the second night of Passover.

Aunt Simcha went, too?

No, Simcha never caught the baseball fever. She was such a serious student. She was in her first year of high school, and she couldn't stand the idea of missing a week of school to go watch baseball, no matter who was about to make history.

A week? It couldn't have taken a week to get to Atlanta and back, even back then.

No, but we couldn't exactly call Mr. Aaron and ask him kindly to hurry up and hit his home run on Monday so the girls could get back to school, now, could we? That's the other reason I was so angry: your grandfather bought tickets to all four baseball games that week, and his plan was to take the girls out of school for the whole week to go sit a home run vigil. Simcha wouldn't go, but Nina, well, I guess with all the questions you've been asking you're starting to get the impression she was a pretty strong-willed girl. Once she knew her dad had tickets, she would have run away and hitchhiked to Atlanta to get to those games.

Did it take the whole week?

As it turned out, Mr. Aaron did not like the idea of Nina's missing school any more than I did—he got his home run in the home opener that Monday night. When Sam and Nina called me—near midnight—to report on the success of their mission, they were none too surprised to hear me order them to get right to sleep and to get themselves home first thing Tuesday.

How do you remember what night it was?

Some things you don't forget. It's not very often in life you pass up the chance to see Babe Ruth's record broken, now, is it? (*She laughs.*)

What's funny, Gigi?

Oh, I was a bit of a pill, wasn't I?

TWO

If Friday hadn't been the worst day of a really awful week, Fig might have been able to keep himself from decking Gus Starks at practice Friday afternoon. He should have known the day was going to stink when he stumbled into the bathroom in the morning and noticed the gigantic zit that had burst forth directly between his eyes. Then there was practically a flash flood on the way to school, ruining the stupid drama club posters he had spent all night Thursday working on. Posters that took hours to create took sixty seconds to turn into a soggy mess.

Rachel couldn't even remember to say thanks when he showed her the messed-up posters in fourth period study hall, and the Wicked Stepsisters just glared at the Mega Zit, which Fig was sure was pulsating like Rudolf's red nose. He should have just called it quits right then and there. His throat was scratchy—an afternoon on the nurse's couch couldn't hurt. But no, the day had to drag on to include getting tripped by his moron of a best friend and thus twisting his ankle on the way into science class, and being late for practice after school because the lunch lady didn't appreciate the cleverness of Fig and Tony using tater tots for a spontaneous table-top shoot out.

By the time Fig and Tony got to the field, practice was well underway. Coach was running the team through a defensive drill in which three guys passed in a triangle, essentially playing keep away from a fourth player in the middle. On the sideline, Fig and Tony did a few stretches, then some passing and juggling.

"Pass it to my left," Fig said. He'd been concentrating all fall on getting better with his left foot. When Tony's next pass came sharply in the direction of Fig's right foot, Fig turned his body and stopped the ball with the outside of his left, then smoothly rolled the ball back across his body. "Other left, moron!" he said, tapping his left thigh for emphasis.

Coach pointedly ignored them. Pretending they didn't exist was his way of punishing them for being late.

When the drill ended, the two boys jogged out to join the others as the team gathered around Coach Lambert. Coach looked at his watch and said, "So glad you guys decided to join us."

"Sorry," they mumbled together.

Coach announced a half-field drill, dividing the team into two squads, one offense, and one defense. Fig's group was on defense first. Their job was to keep the other side from scoring and to get the ball cleanly back to Coach Lambert, who stationed himself at around mid-field. Fig marked Gus, and it didn't take Gus long to find a way to take a poke at him. Just a few minutes into the scrimmage Fig intercepted a pass and was dribbling up the left side when a slashing kick to his right heel sent him skidding to the grass.

"Hey, man!"

"Grow up, dude," Gus retorted before racing down the field with the ball. Fig looked up at Coach, who seemed not to have noticed. Fig popped up and raced toward Gus as fast as he could. Tony had driven Gus into the corner, and the two were banging bodies, scrapping for the ball. Fig ran past them into the corner, so when Tony was able to jar the ball loose from the tangle of feet, Fig was ready to play it along the sideline to Jack, who one-touched it over to Coach. Score one for the defense.

This cat-and-mouse game continued, with the squad playing offense making progress toward the goal until someone was forced to pass to Gus, who was so laser-focused on driving toward the goal that it didn't matter if the defense left a man open on one side or the other, allowing Fig and his teammates to double and triple team him, taking the ball away time after time. The defense had taken control of the ball and returned it to Coach nine or ten times before Gus's side finally slipped a shot past the keeper for a goal.

"Faaace!" Gus shouted, pushing his hand into Fig's face as he trotted past to the center circle.

Coach shouted for a switch, and Fig's squad had a turn at offense. Fig set up Raj and Tony for two goals each before the defense managed a stop. The next time, after dishing a pass to Raj on the left side, Fig broke straight for the upright on the goalie's left, taking a perfectly timed pass back from Raj and stuffing it into the back of the net.

Just as Fig got the shot off, Gus, who had chased him into the fray, barreled into him with the full force of a football tackle. The hit lifted Fig clear off his feet. First his body, then his head slammed into the ground, before Gus landed on top of him, taking his breath away. For a brief moment Fig saw what looked like fireworks behind the blackness of his closed eyelids, and when he opened his eyes, his vision remained blurry for just a moment.

But blurry vision didn't keep him from seeing the stupid grin on Gus's face, and Fig snapped, grabbing the other boy's arm and rolling him over on the grass. Head pounding with pain, Fig flipped himself over, straddling his stunned nemesis. Wheeling from right to left and back again, Fig hammered both sides of Gus's face with punches before the guys were able to pull him off.

Coach Lambert's red face appeared inches from Fig's. "Get off my field! You're done! And don't even think about coming back tomorrow."

"What?" Fig shouted back, still in fight mode.

Coach Lambert stabbed the air in the direction of the sideline.

"But Coach, the game—"

"Out!"

Fig didn't look at anyone as he walked, head down,

toward the parking lot at the edge of the field. He didn't remember Gus landing any punches, but his face burned as if he had been slapped.

THREE

Friday nights were usually Fig's favorite. "Wings and Beer Night" they called it. On Friday nights, Dad would stop on the way home and get a huge order of hot chicken wings and crinkle-cut fries loaded down with melted cheddar, and they'd go home, put a game or an old movie and stuff themselves, washing it all down with root beer.

Not tonight.

When Fig got home from practice, he found his dad in the breezeway between the garage and the rest of the house, surrounded by stacks of newspapers, shoes and dirty laundry.

"Hey."

"Hey, Dad." He dreaded his father's inevitable lecture; it would be best to tell him about the fight immediately. Get it over with. After all, he was going to have to explain why he wasn't going to be in tomorrow's game.

"There was a fight," he began.

He stopped. It hadn't really been a fight. Gus was a real jerk who probably deserved a beating, and he had been playing dirty, but still it wasn't a fight. Fig had blown up and attacked another player. Worse. Attacked a teammate.

Dad wore the thick, hooded Cornell sweatshirt that served as his coat on all but the coldest days. As always, he had a baseball cap on. Today it was the St. Louis Cardinals. "Gus was playing dirty," Fig said, "really rubbing it in. Anyway, I punched him a few times. I'm suspended for tomorrow's game." There. It was out.

Fig's father held up his cell phone. "Coach Lambert called me a few minutes ago."

Why did adults do that? Let you tell them something they already knew? Fig hated that. In the silence that followed, he braced himself for the lecture. He'd gotten more lectures in the six weeks since seventh grade began than in the first twelve years of his life.

Dad would say: "You know better, Fig."

He'd say: "We're not violent people, Fig."

He'd sigh and add: "There's a big difference between being aggressive and fighting."

Fig waited. There was no reason to argue back. What he had done was stupid. It could cost him his place on the team. He would stand patiently and let Dad tell him what he always told him.

Fig could tell his dad was mad, or disappointed or whatever, but he didn't say anything about the fight. Instead, he handed Fig a basket of dirty laundry and said, "We pick Gigi up Sunday morning. By then I want this place to sparkle." He directed Fig to start a load of laundry and to empty the dishwasher then went back to attacking the piles.

"I'll make some mac and cheese?" Fig said, raising his voice up at the end as if he was asking a question.

Dad didn't even look up from his sorting. "Don't worry about me. I'll get some cereal later." Fig ended up eating alone in front of the TV, watching *Return of the Jedi*. It was one of his favorite movies of all time, but he was too irritated to enjoy it. When he finished eating he turned it off and headed up to his room.

He sat down at his desk and pulled out the center drawer. From the tray in the front of the drawer he removed a charcoal pencil, which he sharpened with a small pocketknife. Satisfied with the tip, he reached into the back of the drawer and pulled out a small metal key. The key opened a deep drawer on the left side of his desk. He selected from a pile of sketchbooks a large, hardbound, dark green book. He flipped past pages of sketches until he found a blank page. Immediately he divided the page into four rows with two to four panels per row. Fig had been doing this for so long that, though his hand moved quickly, his lines were clean and carefully placed.

The page now looked like a page from a comic book, but with empty frames. He almost always started this way. Depending on how he was feeling, he would spend more or less time preparing the page before he'd start his first sketch. Sometimes, especially if he had a scene in mind, he would simply divide up the page and start right in on the first panel. At other times, he might spend twenty minutes playing with the shading within the panels or creating fancy-looking borders before drawing any pictures.

Fig was not actually a big fan of comics or graphic novels. Movies were his first love after soccer, and his sketches were more like film scenes—blueprints for movies he'd imagined—than comics. Dialogue didn't come naturally to Fig, and he often simply let the pictures tell the story.

Today, in the small, almost square, opening frame, Fig drew a top-down view of a soccer ball in the center circle of a field, with the toe of a shoe resting atop the ball. The perspective was so close that only part of the ball could be seen in the tight frame. In the next box, a long, rectangular frame, Fig drew a player dribbling the ball down the field defended by two opponents. In this box, the "camera" in Fig's mind pulled back a little, enough to include the lower legs, but no more, of all three players.

By the time he went to bed, he had filled the page with one scene after another. In the final panel, just after a small, square frame filled beyond its borders with the screaming face of Coach Lambert, Fig's father stood amid a pile of laundry, his face a mixture of anger and sadness. Fig put his pencil down and smiled at this portrait. He was getting pretty good at drawing his dad's face.

The next morning, Fig woke up with a pounding headache to a nasty vibrating sound. Maybe the neighbor was running a leaf blower right outside Fig's bedroom window. When the noise stopped suddenly, Fig realized it was the vacuum in the next room.

He didn't see why his dad was freaking out about making the house so perfectly clean for Gigi's unexpected visit. This was a *guy* house. Laundry got done when there was nothing left to wear. Meals were simple: mac and cheese some nights, pizza other nights. Anyway, Gigi wasn't coming to inspect the house. She wasn't even coming to see them. She was coming to go to the hospital.

He leaned over and pulled the curtains open. A steady drizzle coated the window with droplets. Enough to make it gross to be outside, but not enough to interrupt the game. He should be at the field with his team. Instead, today he was stuck here with Mr. Clean.

Why had he been so stupid yesterday? He and Gus had been warned before about fighting. What if Coach kicked him off the team for good? How would he ever make the Elites if he couldn't even keep his spot on this team?

Fig had to pee pretty bad, but as soon as he walked into the hallway he was going to be roped into clean-up duty, so he ignored his bladder and opened a book. He read a few pages, but it was hard to focus. His head was pounding, his vision a bit blurry. The last thing he needed was a concussion. Then again, if Coach did give him the boot, it wouldn't matter if he couldn't play.

His father was now banging dishes in the kitchen sink. And he really did have to use the bathroom. Fig put the book down and rolled out of bed with a groan.

It was going to be a long day.

Tony texted as soon as the game was over: "Enjoying your RED CARD?!?! LOL." By noon, he and Fig were scarfing pizza at Riselli's. For a skinny kid, Tony could eat like a horse. Fig had to eat fast to keep up.

"So, dude, what's the deal?" Tony asked, wiping his mouth with a wad of napkins. "How long you out?"

"I don't know," Fig said. "Coach wants me and my dad to meet with him in his office at 3:45 Monday." Coach Lambert was a PE teacher at one of the elementary schools in town, and he tended to use his office at the school as a makeshift team office after regular school hours.

Tony's eyes lit up. "That's good news—3:45 means he wants to see you right before practice starts. Probably means you're back on, right?"

Fig shrugged.

Tony was chipper. "Dude, if he wanted to kick you off the team, he wouldn't drag your dad down there to do it. He'd have said something on the phone."

There was only one thing Fig could think of that might get him out of his bad mood today.

"Let's make a movie!" he said. Making short movies—most were just scenes, really—was something he and Tony did together from time to time. Back at Tony's house they dug out some old Halloween costumes and started by filming a sword fight, setting Fig's phone on a bookshelf and fighting out in the center of the room, but it ended up looking pretty stupid. They'd made some Lego animation videos in the past, but neither was in the mood today for messing with all the pieces. It was when Tony's mom called them into the kitchen for milk and cookies—she actually made them milk and cookies!—that they stumbled on their breakthrough idea. Tony's sister Erica was sitting at the kitchen table trying to construct various molecules out of modeling clay.

"That's it," Fig burst out. "Claymation!"

"What?" Tony asked.

"We'll make a Claymation video." Turning to Erica he asked, "Can I borrow your laptop for a minute?"

Fig and Tony watched a how-to video on YouTube, then they dove into creating a little clay figure and filming him in a series of actions, one little step at a time. The result was pretty cool.

Fig ended up spending the night at Tony's, and when he got back home Sunday morning, the house was barely recognizable. Piles of newspapers had been either thrown out or hidden. The dining room table—Homework Central for Fig—had been cleared of all papers and covered with a tablecloth and flowers. Even the desk in the extra bedroom downstairs, which Fig's father used as an office, was spotless. And for the first time maybe ever, all the laundry had been washed, folded *and put away* all in the same weekend. Every carpet had been vacuumed, every floor mopped, every bathroom cleaned.

Gigi's plane was delayed due to rainstorms, and Fig was starving by the time she arrived. Gigi walked right up to him and squeezed him hard. She held him by the shoulders and surveyed him up and down. Evidently satisfied with his growth since last spring, she gave him a big smile and announced with a sigh, "Elijah, sweetie."

Gigi was the one person who refused to call her grandson by his nickname.

"I'm sorry, Elijah," she once explained. "Your mother left you with a beautiful name. For her sake, I can't call you by the name of a cookie."

As Fig's father picked up her sole suitcase, Gigi said, "I'm sorry about all this, Jeff. You're dear to have me."

That was the last they spoke of the real reason for her visit, at least in front of Fig. In the car Gigi chatted merrily about seemingly everything else. The flight. The weather in Charleston. Aunt Simcha and the girls. Everything, that is, but doctor appointments and tests. They seemed to have made a silent agreement to pretend that this was just another visit. Fig wasn't sure if this performance was intended for his benefit, but he hated the fakeness of pretending everything was fine when clearly, if she had come all the way to Cleveland for medical tests, everything was not fine.

They didn't go right home. Over the years they had developed a routine. First they went to lunch at a kosher restaurant—Dad and Gigi always argued over who would pay, and Gigi always won. Fig got what he always got: chicken fingers and French fries. When they had gone through the standard questions about school and sports, Fig pulled out his phone and said to Gigi, "Check this out. My first Claymation video. Well, mine and Tony's." He pressed play. "It's only two minutes, but it took *forever* to make."

The screen went from solid blue to grey fuzz. Finally, a handwritten sign in bright green magic marker appeared. "THE SHORT LIFE," it said in all caps.

A hand appeared and pulled the sign off screen, revealing an orange-lettered sign.

"AND TRAGIC DEATH."

Another hand. Now a yellow sign, a bit difficult to read. "OF CLAY MAN."

Fuzz. What followed was the most rudimentary rendition of stop-motion animation imaginable. In each of fifty-seven separate two-second segments of video, a little blue clay figure—two arms, a trunk, and two legs, no head—was posed to imitate a single movement. A step, a movement of an arm. If you pretended not to notice the awkward cuts between each pose you could almost imagine Clay Man moving steadily across Tony's kitchen counter toward a

27

cookie jar, scaling it successfully, and managing in a fleeting moment of glory to push the lid up—ignore the human wrist in the background—only to have it come crashing down on his headless clay torso.

When the animation ended, a violet-lettered sign announced: "WRITTEN AND DIRECTED BY E.S. NEWTON AND ANTONIO CARR."

"E.S. Newton, huh?" his father asked with a broad smile.

"Bravo!" Gigi applauded as if he'd just won an Oscar.

When lunch was over, they went to the kosher butcher and grocery. Fig always felt awkward in this store. All the men there wore yarmulkes and fringes under their shirts. As they entered the store Fig's father removed the Cincinnati Reds cap he had chosen for today; Fig left his own Cleveland cap on.

Gigi had been shopping there for years, and even though she only came in once or twice a year, the woman behind the cash register greeted her with a big smile.

"Greta! Baruch Ha-Shem!" she announced, thanking God for the pleasure of seeing her again. She turned to her husband behind the meat counter. "Schmuel," she shouted. "Look, it's Greta. From Charleston."

The butcher wiped his hands and waved, smiling widely, but his wife did the talking. "What brings you here in this cold weather?"

Gigi did not drop the big smile with which she had greeted the storekeepers, but it seemed to Fig that she had pulled a thin shield over her face.

"Could I ever see enough of this handsome young man?" she asked, looking over at Fig. "Look how fast he's growing. If I stay away too long, I'll miss it all."

The woman smiled at Fig, who politely turned up the corners of his mouth. He grabbed a newspaper off the rack and re-read the sports section while Gigi selected groceries.

"Tons of homework," Fig announced the moment they got home, taking the steps up to his bedroom two at a time. He probably did have a lot of homework, but he had left his book bag in his locker at school. He would have to catch up during study hall Monday. His head felt a little numb, and the feeling in the pit of his stomach was still there. He tried to return to his drawing, but it was hard to concentrate, so when the smells of Gigi's cooking reminded him he was hungry, he was glad to abandon it and head downstairs. The table was set with matching lavender paper plates and plastic silverware. Gigi kept kosher, which meant, among other things, that she didn't eat pork or shrimp, and she didn't mix milk and meat in the same meal. It also meant she made a big deal out of not eating off plates that had ever had ham or bacon on them. So when Gigi came to visit, they did not eat off their own dishes. He didn't understand why those rules were so important to her, but her delicious cooking usually made up for the inconvenience.

Fig, who couldn't stop thinking about the next day's meeting with Coach Lambert, barely said a word during dinner. His father and Gigi didn't seem to notice, content to continue their fake happy chatter from earlier. When he had finished eating, Fig got up and took a gallon of vanilla ice cream out of the freezer. As he opened the drawer for a spoon, his father gave him a sharp look and pointed to the chicken on the platter in front of them.

"Milk and meat."

Fig rolled his eyes and put the ice cream back into the freezer. He headed out of the kitchen.

"How about clearing your plate and thanking Gigi for a nice meal?" Dad demanded.

Fig piled his lavender knife, fork and napkin onto his plate and dropped them on the kitchen counter. Stopping at the doorway, he said, "Thanks, Gigi. It was delicious." He gave his dad a smirk. "A lot better than the stuff this guy makes—when he cooks." And he was off.

As he headed for the stairs, he heard his father say, "What can I say, Greta? I guess manners aren't what we focus on around here."

Fig spent the rest of the evening in his room pretending to do homework. He ended up reading instead. When he turned off his light at nine o'clock, he could still hear his father and Gigi chatting in the living room. How could anyone just sit around and talk for hours? Fig didn't even brush his teeth or come down to say goodnight.

As if things weren't bad enough with school and the bar mitzvah stuff, now he had to worry about his grandmother having to get these medical tests. And tomorrow afternoon

Coach was probably going to kick him out of the only thing he was any good at. He tossed and turned for over an hour after he had turned his light off.

FOUR

When Fig's alarm went off Monday morning, he had already been awake for a while. He was going over and over in his mind, trying to figure out the best way to convince Coach to keep him on the team.

His dad usually left for the dental clinic early, and Fig was used to having the house to himself in the morning, so when he flew into the kitchen for a quick bite, he was startled to see Gigi sitting at the table sipping coffee and reading the newspaper.

"Can I make you some breakfast, Elijah, sweetie?" she asked, standing up.

"No time," he said, stuffing two packets of granola bars into his jacket pocket. "But thanks anyway." He raced out the door, where Tony and his mom were waiting to pick him up.

"No book bag?" Mrs. Carr asked as Fig got into the mini-van. She never acted like she was trying to replace Fig's mother, but she couldn't help acting motherly.

Fig shrugged sheepishly. "I left it at school Friday." She

shook her head and sighed, but the look on her face was soft. Worried, not judging.

Fig managed to slide through the morning without much hassle. In English, he bluffed his way through the discussion of the balcony scene from *Romeo and Juliet*. Fig had no idea why teachers thought it was a good idea to teach Shakespeare to seventh graders, but since he was stuck with the only seventh grade English teacher in America who hadn't heard that no one diagrams sentences anymore, he enjoyed those days when they actually discussed a story.

In his next class he quickly scribbled out his French homework in the back of class while the teacher told some elaborate story—entirely in French—about nobody knew what. Mr. Barne liked to start off each class this way. He said it was okay if no one understood a word he said, that he was training their ears, and that over time, as they learned more and more vocabulary, they'd begin to catch on. Hadn't happened yet.

There had been a test on Friday in American history, so there was no homework there, and fourth period band was mellow, giving Fig a chance to get his algebra homework done.

By lunchtime, he was feeling pretty good.

Eating with Robert, who hated soccer, made it easier to avoid thinking about soccer. Fig and Tony had been eating with Robert since the second week of school. Robert was new this year, and except for the fact that he hated soccer, he was a great guy. Robert played basketball, but his obsession was girls. As soon as Fig set down his tray of mystery burger, mushy French fries and chocolate milk, Robert started giving a running commentary on the relative cuteness of all the girls in the cafeteria.

Tony was too busy stuffing his face to say much, and Fig was in no mood for stupid banter, but that didn't stop Robert. Fig wondered whether, if he and Tony weren't there, Robert would have kept on talking anyway. Probably. But Robert was a good kid, and usually pretty funny. Usually.

"So, Figgie, I saw Rachel give you the cold shoulder in study hall. You two having a lovers' quarrel?"

"You know what, dude?" Tony stuffed a handful of fries into Robert's open mouth. "You talk too much, you know that?"

"I'm just saying, if you like her, you ought to ask her to go out with you."

Fig sighed. The *second* last thing in the world Fig wanted to talk about was asking Rachel Friedman to go out with him. But at least it took his mind off the *very* last thing in the world he wanted to talk about, which was his meeting with Coach—in less than four hours.

When the bell rang to signal the end of the lunch period, Fig went to his locker to gather his things for the afternoon classes. Just science, study hall and art. Thank goodness for study hall and art at the end of the day. Study hall gave him a chance to get his homework started, and art was usually fun.

Fig grabbed his science textbook and riffled through a mass of folders, binders, and loose papers wedged between the little shelf above the coat hook and the top of the locker. He opened a pale blue folder. French. He opened another. Math. And some diagrammed sentences. Organization was not really Fig's thing. Looking at his watch, he grabbed a small assortment of other folders—science would be in there somewhere—and forced his locker door shut.

He was just turning the corner toward the science wing when the late bell rang.

Oh, no. Mrs. Kaminsky.

Mrs. Kaminsky, Fig's science teacher, had a heavy Russian accent and a stern face. And when she was mad her eyes bored into you like lasers. As he quickened his pace to a trot, Fig could picture the next scene. When he walked into the classroom, Mrs. Kaminsky would stop what she was doing, dramatically suck in a little air as if taken completely by surprise, and glare over the rims of her glasses at him. "Mr. Newton," she would call him. "I certainly hope you have a late pass." Most teachers only called a student "Mr." or "Miss" when they were mad, but since Mrs. Kaminsky referred to everyone that way, she always seemed mad.

When he stepped into the classroom, she was nowhere to be seen. He breathed a sigh of relief. My lucky day, he thought. Get through this class and I'm home free. *Until three forty-five, anyway, when Coach Lambert might kick me off the team.* He quickly moved toward his seat in the back of the room. He was just about to slide into the chair when Mrs. Kaminsky emerged from behind a row of shelves stacked high with cardboard boxes of lab equipment. She gasped dramatically, just as Fig had imagined.

"Mr. Newton, I certainly hope—"

He cut her off, shaking his head from side to side. "No. Sorry, I—" As there was no actual excuse to offer, Fig didn't even finish his sentence. He never knew what to say in these situations.

Rolling her eyes toward the fluorescent lights above, Mrs. Kaminsky took a deep breath. "Please take your seat, Mr. Newton, and pass your lab report quickly to the front of the room. We have a great deal to do today."

Lab report? Oh, man. He'd forgotten all about that assignment. He should have known it was too much to hope he'd be able to get through the whole day without something going wrong. His mind raced. He flipped through the notebooks in his book bag. He could turn in an old lab report, finish the assignment tonight, and then play dumb when confronted with his "mistake." Mrs. Kaminsky thought he was so scatterbrained that he could probably convince her he had accidently turned in the wrong report.

Fig rejected the idea. As much as he hated being singled out in class, he hated cheaters even more.

Mrs. Kaminsky was moving across the front of the classroom, collecting four or five lab reports from the first desk in each row. Fig decided to scribble a quick note of apology, explaining about the forgotten book bag and promising the report first thing tomorrow. But before he had time to do so, she had arrived at the front of his row and was leafing through the pile of reports she'd just collected. He could feel his cheeks growing warm, and his right eye began to sting a little.

"I'm really sorry, Mrs. Kaminsky," he croaked weakly. "I forgot my book bag at school over the weekend. Can I—"

"No lab report?" the teacher shrieked, cutting him off. It seemed that he rarely finished a sentence in her presence. "Again? My goodness, Mr. Newton, *where* is your head?"

It was tempting to make a joke of her question, looking around for his lost head, or answering the question literally. "Well, it's right here on my neck, Mrs. Kaminsky." Sarcasm didn't always translate for her. Some of the boys made a little game out of seeing if they could get her to respond literally to something they had meant sarcastically. Fig just shrank down in his seat and held her stare until finally, mercifully, she turned toward the chalkboard.

Still unable to locate his science notebook, he opened a green spiral notebook and flipped past pages of "-er" verbs and math problems until he found a blank page. He wrote "Life Science" and the date at the top of the page and began to take notes as quickly as he could. He tried hard to listen intently, and he diligently copied down anything Mrs. Kaminsky wrote on the board. But sometimes she would just go on and on for several minutes without writing anything on the board, and during these stretches Fig's mind wandered.

What was Coach going to say after school, anyway? He could handle Coach Lambert yelling at him in front of his dad. He deserved it. He could handle an embarrassing lecture from his dad in front of Coach Lambert. He supposed he'd earned that, too. He was prepared to apologize—in front of the whole team if he had to. What he couldn't handle was being kicked off the team. He tried to imagine what he would do if he couldn't play soccer, but he couldn't picture anything. Soccer was just about the *only* thing he was good at. Just ask Mrs. Kaminsky.

"Mr. Newton?" His name was being called in a sing-songy Russian voice. "Yoo-hoo, Mr. Newton?"

Fig looked up and rubbed his right eye.

"Young man, you are living in a bubble! Everyone else in the room is thinking about the parts of a cell, Mr. Newton. Is it so hard to focus on science for the few minutes we have together?"

He was pretty sure she didn't want an answer to that question. He kept his eyes trained on hers and did his best to ignore the chuckles of his classmates.

Mercifully, the bell rang. Notebooks slammed shut and students pressed themselves into a cluster around the door. Fig quickly piled his things into his book bag and tried to blend in with the departing group.

"Elijah—stay." He wheeled around, surprised to hear his real first name. Mrs. Kaminsky was perched on the corner of her desk, wiping her glasses on a white handkerchief. Without her glasses on she looked younger, some might even say pretty. At the same time, he could see the deep lines around her eyes more clearly. She looked tired. And a little sad.

Looking up at him, she sighed. "I don't know what to do with you," she said. "I'm running out of ideas. Sometimes I think it's going to take having you assigned to my room for a study hall to get you to do your science homework."

"Probably wouldn't hurt," Fig blurted out without thinking.

Mrs. Kaminsky seemed to be weighing whether he was being serious or not.

"Really?" she asked, tentative, studying him.

He shrugged. Why not? It would be hard to forget to do his homework if his teacher was watching him do it.

"Well, then. When is your study hall?" Her voice was decisive, her teacher voice again.

"I'm about to be late for it right now."

"Very well, Mr. Newton," said Mrs. Kaminsky, quickly shoving her glasses back onto her nose. "Sit right down and begin working on that lab report. I'll go let the study hall monitor know you'll be spending this period with me for the time being. When I return, I've got some work of my own to do, but I expect you to have two or three intelligent questions for me about what you've been asked to do."

With that, she promptly turned and left the room.

Two periods a day with Mrs. Kaminsky. What had he

gotten himself into? And if Coach ended up kicking him off the team, he might as well just give up and move to Siberia or something.

REMEMBERING NINA
Interview with Jeffrey Allen Newton

Please state your full name.

Jeffrey Allen Newton.

Relationship to Nina?

Would it kill you to say "Mom"?

It's a documentary, Dad.

(*Sighing.*) Husband.

So, where did you go on your first date?

Hmmmm ... good question. Our first date ...

You don't remember your first date?

It's not that simple. You see, we could never quite agree which date was our first. Soon after we met, your mother invited me to join her and a few other friends to hear a lecture. Afterward, the friends suddenly announced they had to be somewhere, and we ended up having coffee and talking for a couple hours. I thought she had planned it that way, and I always counted that as our first date.

But Nina?

Well, I had so much fun at coffee that I called her the next day and invited her to go see a movie. *Bull Durham,* actually. It's a baseball movie. She always insisted that was the first date. And you really shouldn't call her Nina.

Did you get a smooch after the coffee?

Excuse me?

First kiss. Did you kiss her after the coffee or after the movie?

It's not mandatory—or necessarily preferable—to kiss on a first date. Two people who are getting to know each other can enjoy a date without kissing.

Thanks for the info, Dad. I'll be sure to feature it prominently in the "parental advice" section of the finished documentary. Are you going to answer the question?

Well, Mr. Smarty Pants, if you must know, our first kiss did happen on the evening we went to see *Bull Durham.* When I dropped her off at the door, just like in the movies.

So she was right.

What?

Nina was right. The coffee thing wasn't really a date.

FIVE

"Coulda used you in the game Saturday," Coach Lambert growled when they met in his cramped office after school. His nose and cheeks seemed to reflect the red of his flaming hair. His eyes bored into Fig's. "You made a bad call, Newton."

Fig looked down at his feet, then at his father, who nodded earnestly. Then he looked into his coach's eyes. "I'm sorry. It was wrong to—"

Coach cut him off. "You know I can't have a player taking shots at a teammate."

Fig's heart raced. This was the moment. He really didn't know what he'd do if Coach kicked him off the team.

"It just ain't right," Coach continued. His dad's most serious face punctuated the coach's criticism of his son. Fig knew his father was happy to hear Coach Lambert giving him such a hard time. "Even if the other guy does deserve a good whacking."

Did he detect a hint of a smile curl Coach's lips? His heart leapt. Even *Coach* thought Gus was a jerk. He just couldn't say so. Maybe he was going to give Fig a second chance after all.

Coach took off his ball cap, ran a hand through his thinning red hair, and leaned forward with a very serious look on his face. "Now, I need the two of you to understand that I've given this a lot of thought," he continued. "Wrestled with it all weekend, in fact."

Oh, no. Here it came. He was going to do it. He was really going to kick Fig off the team.

"Coach, I—" Fig started to say. Coach held a hand up.

"Let me finish what I've got to say here, Fig," he commanded. "You've got a lot of potential, son."

Fig held his breath. Coach paused for what seemed like a very long time.

"One more incident like this, and you're tying my hands." Coach held up his hands in front of his face, wrists together as if handcuffed. "Understand?"

Was he hearing right? He wasn't off the team? He wasn't off the team! It was all he could do to keep from whooping as he said, "Yes, sir."

"Now go warm up while I talk to Dad. We got a lot to do tonight."

"Thanks, Coach," he said. "Thanks a lot." He avoided eye contact with his father and practically skipped out of the coach's office to the field.

His teammates were as thrilled as he was.

"Gus is a total jerk," said Joey D., a wicked defender and usually a soft-spoken kid. "He was asking for it."

"Bingo," Tony agreed.

"It's about time you showed some muscle out there," said Simmy, their goalie and the biggest guy on the team by about twenty pounds.

At that afternoon's practice, Fig felt more confident than ever, seeing the field more clearly and directing traffic up and down like this was *his* team. With Gus gone, the other guys seemed to be looking to Fig to be more of a leader.

Fig's father stayed on and watched practice. As they walked out to the car together, Fig was ecstatic.

"Didya see me?" he asked. "I was, like, totally in the zone out there."

"You played great," Dad agreed.

"It's so much better with Gus outta here," he said. "I shoulda smacked him a long time ago."

"Now, Fig!" The disappointed parent voice. "There's a difference between being aggressive and fighting. Especially with your own teammates."

"Well, he's not my teammate anymore." He stared at his father, ready to defend himself. His father kept his eyes on the road and said nothing. His dad wasn't like Fig. He wasn't a fighter. Fig didn't expect him to understand. He dropped the subject. Nothing was going to spoil his good mood.

As they entered the house through the garage, Fig was hit with two sensations: One was the absence of clutter in the breezeway. The other was the smell of something wonderful on the stove. Gigi! In all the worry of the day, then the excitement of practice, he had almost forgotten she was here.

He dropped his sports bag, kicked off his shoes, and bounded into the kitchen.

"I sure could get used to having real dinners around here," he declared, playfully wrapping his arms around Gigi before opening the fridge for a Gatorade. "What's cookin'?"

"I've made a pot roast," she said with a smile. "It's a month closer to winter up here. I wanted something to warm our bones a little."

Dad came into the kitchen and gave Gigi a peck on the check.

"You're going to spoil us, Greta," he said.

She smiled her quiet smile. "I'll do my best."

Then she turned to Fig. "Dinner won't be ready for another thirty minutes. Let's you and I take a walk, Elijah, sweetie."

The suggestion took Fig by surprise. Even with the jump-start he had gotten under Mrs. Kaminsky's eagle eye, he had a fair amount of homework tonight.

"Great idea," his father piped in. He removed the Orioles cap he was wearing and set it on the kitchen counter. "I'll set the table."

"Sure," said Fig. How often did he get to see Gigi in October, right?

Gigi threw a sweater over her shoulders, and they headed out. It was a clear evening, but Gigi was right. There was a hint of winter in the air. Now that Fig had cooled down from practice, he was chilly in his sweat-drenched shirt. He put his hands in the pockets of his jeans.

"Which way?" he asked.

She looped her hand into the crook of Fig's arm in an old-fashioned way and nodded her head to the right. "You sure seem pleased with yourself tonight," Gigi said. "What news?" This was her way of asking what was up.

"Practice was awesome!" Fig grinned. "With Gus gone it was like my team. I was in charge out there. Totally in the zone. Everybody says we're better off without Gus."

Gigi laughed and tugged at his arm. "Slow down. It feels like we're about to take off." Fig slowed his pace.

"Now, who's this Gus of whom everyone is so happy to be rid?"

"Oh, just this ball hog no one likes," Fig said. "He was called up to take this boy Georgie's place on the Elites after he got his third concussion."

"Whoa! Slow down. What is 'Elites'"?

"It's a traveling team, just like my team. But it's, like, the next level up."

"Like?" Gigi despised the unnecessary use of the word "like" by the younger generation.

"It *is* the next level up."

"I see. And Georgie played in this league but now has a concussion." She seemed intent on memorizing the details.

"Yeah, smacked heads pretty good with another kid. The other kid was fine, but Georgie went out cold. Doctor said he's out for the school year and probably shouldn't play ever again, which would totally suck."

He gave Gigi an apologetic look. "Stink," he corrected himself.

Gigi just smiled.

"Anyway, tryouts are only in the spring. Two guys from our team made the Elites last spring, but me and Gus didn't."

"Until now," Gigi said, connecting the dots. "Now Gus has been called up to replace Georgie."

"Yeah, but he's no better than me." Fig felt the anger all over again. "He's bigger is all. And he's an expert at elbowing someone's ribs under the radar."

The temperature was dropping steadily, and an occasional spit of drizzle struck their faces. Gigi seemed unconcerned about the possibility of getting caught in the rain.

"You will have another chance to try out for these Elites next spring?" she asked.

"Yeah. The coach is a friend of Coach Lambert's, and he told Coach Lambert with a little more size and strength I should have a pretty good shot."

"I am confident you'll make the team you want to make next spring—if you continue to work very hard."

"I hope so."

"I *know* so," she continued. "In the end, the more talented player always shines over a dirty player with less talent."

Somehow hearing it from Gigi made it seem a little more

real, more possible. Parents have to say encouraging stuff to their kids, but one thing about Gigi, you always knew that if she said something, she meant it.

"I'd like to see you play sometime, Elijah," she said.

"You're not a soccer fan, Gigi."

"You're right. I'm not," she said. "But it's important to me because it's important to you."

He liked that. They had walked all the way around the block and were back at the bottom of Fig's driveway. Before turning up the driveway, Gigi stopped and let go of Fig's arm.

"Thank you for a lovely walk," she said. And then, as if continuing the conversation they'd been having, but in a slightly softer voice, Gigi said, "Elijah, sweetheart, I got some pretty tough news at the hospital today."

Oh, man. He had completely forgotten that today was the day Gigi had gone to Great Lakes for her tests.

"I hate to be the bearer of sad tidings," she continued. "But I asked your dad to let me be the one to tell you."

She smiled her peaceful smile. They might as well have been talking about her plans for her flower garden for next spring, or his eldest cousin Shoshana's new job.

"The doctors told me I've got—"

Fig put up his hands between them as if to fend off a punch. He wasn't sure if he was ready to hear what she was about to say. Gigi seemed to sense his anxiety and kept the last word to herself for a moment. Fig's head felt clouded, and he realized he was very tired. The cool of the evening had crept inside his jacket and clung to his ribs. He needed a shower. He had work to do. He pulled his jacket more snugly to his body.

"The doctors say I have cancer, sweetie. Pretty far along."

Fig looked closely at his mother's mother. He snapped a mental picture of Gigi at that moment. The strong moonlight caught the strands of grey in her straight black hair. When had Gigi's hair turned so grey? How could she always be so calm? About everything?

"Scared?" He could only manage the one word.

Gigi answered calmly, without hesitation. "It's an awful disease," she said. "I watched what it did to your mother. Who wouldn't be scared?"

Fig had been only four years old when his mother died of cancer. He remembered very little about her, and he remembered nothing about her struggle with the disease. It must have been horrible for Gigi to watch her daughter suffer.

But she didn't sound scared. She sounded like the heroine in an old movie.

She smiled. "Let's go eat. I've made a nice supper."

Fig didn't feel much like eating, but he nodded and headed up the driveway.

REMEMBERING NINA
Interview with Jeffrey Allen Newton

Are you ready for a really tough one?

Anything. Try me.

How did you first discover that my mother had cancer?

Whoa! (*Long pause.*) No, I guess I'm not ready for that one. (*Long pause.*) Please turn the camera off. Sorry, chief.

SIX

"It's not fair!"

His father looked over from the driver's seat. They were on the way to the synagogue for class.

"I'm sorry, chief," Dad said, adjusting the Blue Jays cap he was wearing today. "It would make Gigi uncomfortable, and I'm not willing to do that right now."

Gigi had gone back to South Carolina to pack some more things and to put her house in order. She and her doctors at Great Lakes had decided to try an aggressive treatment, a treatment that would mean she'd be sick a lot for a while. They didn't know for how long, but for the time being, she was going to be staying with them.

Fig had been upset all week. Everything in his entire life was going wrong. And now, on the way to class, his dad had announced that this year they'd have no Christmas tree.

"*Everybody* has a tree!" he shouted. "It's not about Jesus, Dad. Bobby Jones is an *atheist*. *He* has a tree. *He* gets presents on Christmas."

When his father said nothing, Fig pressed the argument further.

"Dad, it's not even really a *Christian* holiday anymore. It's an *American* holiday. *Everyone* celebrates Christmas." Fig could hear the childishness in his own voice, but he didn't care. They had had a Christmas tree for as long as he could remember.

"We can go over to Aunt Jean's on Christmas," Dad offered. "And I'm sure if you wanted, we could go over early and help them decorate."

Aunt Jean was his dad's sister, mother of the evil twins Jodi and Rita.

"Oh, that'll be fun," Fig said sarcastically.

"Look, Fig, we've got bigger things to worry about than whether or not you get a tree this year." His father's voice was rising. "I never should have let us have a tree in the first place."

"Yeah, well, then why did you?" Fig demanded, his temper flaring.

"I don't like your attitude!" His dad was yelling now. He almost never yelled. "You're not a child anymore. And you know what you're being? You're being selfish."

Fig said nothing. If he kept his mouth shut, maybe his father would lose steam. No such luck. He was going on about how Fig really needed to "apply" himself. School. Homework. Grades. The full lecture.

As they turned into the parking lot, his father said, "You know, the world doesn't revolve around Elijah Samuel

Newton." He was on a roll now. "That's your problem, you know. All you think about is you. What *you* need—or *think* you need. What *you* want. *When* you want it. Well, that's not how the world works. We all have to do things we don't want to, and the sooner you learn that, the better off we'll all be."

Fig stared pointedly out the window. Through the leafless trees he could see the floodlit face of the synagogue. Now, coming to a stop in front of the building, his father added learning Hebrew to the list of things Fig needed to work harder at. "It's time you started taking responsibility for yourself."

Fig could hold his tongue no longer. "This whole bar mitzvah thing was your idea, not mine," he blurted.

"If you'd give this class a chance, maybe you'd—"

"Just because *she* was Jewish doesn't mean I'm gonna be," Fig cut him off.

His father was stunned in mid-sentence. His mouth hung open. It was an unfair weapon, Fig knew. If they had been fighting with swords, Fig had just wielded a lightsaber. He hadn't meant to be hurtful, but all this talk of religion made him uncomfortable.

Finally his father spoke. "See you at eight," he said quietly.

Fig nodded and got out of the car. The car door shut with a louder bang than he had intended. He hesitated, thought about opening it back up to explain he hadn't meant to slam it. Instead, he raised a hand in a half-wave. His father nodded. No smile. Fig turned and walked into the synagogue.

REMEMBERING NINA
Interview with Jeffrey Allen Newton

So what made you fall in love with Nina?

Her kindness. And her intelligence. And her beauty—she had the most amazing eyes. If someone says "grey eyes" you don't think "Wow!", but Nina had these piercing eyes—like gun-metal grey—and when she looked at you with those eyes, you just wanted to do whatever she asked.

Wow.

Yeah. Wow is right. She was really something. Oh—and seeing her in a baseball cap for the first time. That sealed the deal. No one has ever looked cuter in a ball cap.

I've never heard you talk about her that way before.

You've never asked before.

(Long pause.) Actually, you never talk about her at all, Dad. You just get that look on your face when something makes you think of her, but you don't talk.

I'm sorry about that. That's not fair to you, is it? Tell you what, anytime you want to know anything, just ask.

That's not what I mean. You should just talk about her more. You know, when something makes you think of her, say what's on your mind ... Why are you laughing?

You wouldn't want me to start talking every time I think of Nina. We'd never talk about anything else.

SEVEN

In November, soccer moved indoors, and Thanksgiving weekend always featured the biggest indoor tournament of the season. Teams came from as far away as Toledo and Youngstown to play. Fig had two games Friday, two games Saturday, and if they won, a championship game on Sunday. Gigi had never been to one of Fig's games. Most were on Saturdays, and while Gigi never harped on him about it, he figured she probably didn't approve of playing soccer on Shabbat, the Jewish day of rest. In fact, since she had come back from gathering her things in South Carolina, she was in the habit of spending the Sabbath at the home of an observant friend. "It gets me out of your hair for a little while," she explained. It also guaranteed her an easy walk to temple and a soccer- and video-game-free Shabbat.

The Thanksgiving weekend tournament started on Friday morning, so it was a perfect opportunity for Gigi to come see a game. They'd been talking about it for a while, but it had not been the easiest week for Gigi. She had received the first of her chemotherapy treatments on Monday, and its effects took everyone by surprise. Gigi kept mostly to her room for two solid days. It was strange to see her so weak. Ordinarily, Gigi dressed very nicely, and usually by the time Fig left for school, so it was weird this week to see her lying around in her bathrobe when he got home from school.

For as long as Fig could remember they had gone to Aunt Jean's for Thanksgiving dinner, and although Gigi was up and dressed by the time Fig stumbled out of bed on Thursday morning, she said she wasn't feeling up to a crowd. Fig's dad suggested they stay home, have a quiet Thanksgiving, just the three of them, but Gigi insisted they go without her. Fig was relieved when, after much debate, his father finally agreed to go. Thanksgiving for three sounded extremely depressing. As it turned out, even though they didn't usually celebrate Thanksgiving with Gigi, going without her turned out to be pretty depressing too.

Happily, the next morning, when Fig cruised into the kitchen to eat breakfast before the tournament, Gigi was already at the breakfast table eating her toast, her hands wrapped around a steaming mug of coffee.

"Good morning," she greeted him. "I'm excited to see you play today."

Fig poured his first bowl of Cocoa Puffs. "You sure you're up for it, Gigi?"

"I can cheer with the best of them." Gigi took a sip of

her coffee. She had a distant look on her face, as though she were lost in thought. Then she said, "When your grandfather was alive, we would go down to the Braves game in Atlanta three or four times a year. You should have heard him whoop it up. You would have enjoyed going to a ball game with Papa."

Strangely, she didn't seem sad when she spoke of her husband, who had died shortly before Fig was born and whose name was Fig's middle name, Samuel. In fact, talking about him always made Gigi seem happy.

When Fig finished his third bowl of cereal, he gave Gigi a peck on the cheek.

"Games start at 9:30 and 1:30," he said. "Take your pick. Dad'll be at both. He'll be happy to drive you to either."

Gigi kissed him back. "Break a leg."

"Huh?"

"Good luck," she explained.

The first game was a blowout. Starting at center-mid, Fig scored two goals and had two assists in a 5–1 win. He stayed hot into the opening minutes of the second game, when an early penalty led to a free kick that Fig buried from eighteen yards out. It was a crazy shot, but he was in the zone. The ball sailed past the fingertips of the diving keeper on the far side of the goal.

The other side, a team from Youngstown, responded immediately, slipping through a surprised defense for a quick strike in the sixth minute. It was the last goal either side would score for a long time. The guys from Youngtown were smaller, but they were more physical than the earlier opponents, and they were very disciplined passers. Fig tried everything he could to help his team go ahead. Taking outside shots, taking inside shots, dishing passes to every attacker on the team. But nothing was going in. The game had ground into a defensive war. The team that could hold out the longest would win.

With the half drawing to a close, Fig spotted an opportunity and took a chance. When the opponents' right halfback sent a soft pass back to his own keeper, Fig left his man and darted at the ball as it rolled toward the goalie's feet. A perfect slide tackle later Fig was back up on his feet with nothing but turf between himself and the goal, but before he could dump the ball into the back of the net, the ref blew the whistle and ran over to get in Fig's face.

"No sliding indoors, kid," the ref, a balding man with a big beer belly, barked. "C'mon. You know better."

Jogging back into position to defend the free kick, Fig realized he'd picked up a nice turf burn on his elbow. He was also tired, so he was relieved a moment later when the whistle blew to signal the end of the first half. Fig glanced over to the bleachers on the opposite sideline, and Gigi gave him a big wave. He wished she had come to the first game instead, a better game for a non-fan. He gave her a quick nod, then hustled over to the bench.

Neither team scored for the first thirty-one minutes of a very physical second half, but with less than four minutes left on the clock, the kid Fig was marking slipped past him on a dead run, caught up to a perfect through-ball from the left side, and one-touched it past Simmy into the net. Just like that it was 2–1.

Fig was determined to tie it up. These other guys weren't better than Fig's team; they were just playing harder down the stretch. "Come on, guys," he shouted as his team set up to restart play. "Let's get one back."

Fig's frustration increased when a sloppy pass from Joey D. led to a turnover, and once again Fig's man was pushing up the field toward Simmy. There was only one thing to do. Fig put his exhausted legs into overdrive and raced after his opponent. At just the right moment, Fig leaned into his man—not hard enough to draw a whistle, just hard enough to slow him down a step—and slipped a foot in to take the ball away. Ball secured, Fig stopped dead, turning slightly outside to keep his body between his opponent and the ball. The other boy's momentum carried him a few steps past Fig, who quickly turned and sent the ball up the sideline to Dieter, who was wide open in the left corner. Dieter sent a beautiful cross pass in to Tony, who lunged at the ball, heading it into the ground at the keeper's feet. The goalie dropped to his knees to try to swallow up the shot, but the ball ricocheted off his body right back into the traffic jam that had gathered in front of the net. Tony tapped it across to Fig, who left-footed it easily past the scrambling keeper to tie the game with just under a minute left to play!

When the other team restarted play, this time it was Fig's team that managed a quick steal. When Raj flipped it to Fig, Fig heard Simmy's dad shouting "THIRTY-FIVE SECONDS! Thirty-four! … Thirty-three! …" After that he heard nothing. He forgot about the coach, the crowd, this morning's win. There was no question in Fig's mind who would take this final shot of the game. No doubt that it would go in. Fig saw himself as if in a movie—he was locked in. Faking right, then left, he shook the last defender. He faked a windup for a hard shot, then floated a butterfly on a perfect arc just over the fingertips of the leaping keeper. Goal!

Fig raised both arms above his head in celebration, and as his teammates mobbed him, the ref blew the final whistle.

Tony fought his way through the pack. "Hat trick, dude!" he shouted, high-fiving Fig. Sure enough, he'd scored the elusive hat trick—three goals in a single game. In fact, he'd scored five goals on the day! If only Coach Green, the coach of the Elite team, could have seen him today. Unfortunately, the Elites were playing in a different tournament, out of town. Oh, well.

Fig jogged over to the sideline to thank his father and Gigi for coming.

"Well done, Elijah, sweetie! That was quite a display of offensive prowess," Gigi said. Her words brought a smile to Fig's face for two reasons. One, he was delighted that she had gotten to see such a good game, and two, who would say something like "offensive prowess" but Gigi?

"Thanks," he said. She opened her arms for a hug, but he pulled back. "You don't want to hug me, I'm—" how had he heard her say it—"I'm 'lathered in perspiration.'"

"Get over here. If you think I'm going to let a little sweat keep me from hugging my soccer star, you've got another think coming." She winked and put a little added emphasis on the word "sweat" to let Fig know she'd caught him having fun with her more formal mode of speaking.

Fig's father, who had on a pale blue button-down shirt, settled for a fist bump.

"Hey, Dad, everyone's going to Riselli's for pizza. Can I go?"

"Sure. Have fun."

It was hard to imagine anything making Riselli's pizza taste better, but being the guy who had scored five goals sure didn't hurt. The guys were chowing down on pizza and recounting the highlights of the game when Fig heard Simmy shout, "Hey, Rachel! You should have seen this guy!" Fig's head shot up and he quickly wiped pizza sauce off his chin. Rachel Friedman and two of the three Wicked Stepsisters had just come into the pizza shop. Fig nearly died when Simmy, on his feet and with his arm around Rachel, embarrassingly bragged about Fig's five goals. Rachel smiled politely and said, "Way to go, Fig," before ducking out from under the goalie's huge arm and following the hostess to a booth.

"*Way to go, Fig,*" Tony and Dieter repeated together in a high-pitched whisper that evidently was supposed to sound like a girl's voice, and when Simmy sat back down, Fig punched him, hard.

"Hey, what was that for?" Simmy asked, rubbing his upper arm as if the big galoot could even feel a punch from Fig. "Just trying to help you out with your girlfriend."

"Shut up, Simmy," Fig whispered angrily.

"*Shut up, Simmy,*" Tony and Dieter echoed, all mock-girl again.

"Hey, look, your mom's here to pick you up," Fig said, pointing behind Tony. Tony took the bait and Fig reached over and took a slice of pizza right off Tony's plate.

It was a good day to be Fig.

REMEMBERING NINA
Interview with Simcha Ruth Block

Thank you for agreeing to participate in this documentary. Please state your full name.

Simcha Ruth Block.

What is your relationship to Nina?

You really shouldn't keep calling her "Nina."

I'm sorry, what would you like me to call her?

"Mom" would be nice. Or at least "my mother."

Okay, please state the nature of your relationship to "my mother."

Your mother was my younger sister. There were just the two of us.

So, were you and your sister close growing up?

When we were very little we used to play together a lot. You know, dolls and such. It's funny, now that I think of it, even then I was the schoolteacher and Nina would be school nurse. I guess it was later she discovered her passion for teeth.

When you were no longer "very little"?

By junior high, I guess, we got less close. Different friends and all. We were very different.

How were you different?

Well Nina was always a faster mover, I guess you could say. Even though I was two years older, Nina always had more friends, even in my class. I was the shy one. Nina was so pretty. So confident. She always had a million …

What? A million what?

Sorry. I was going to say boyfriends, but I'm not sure I should be talking to her son about her old boyfriends.

I promise I won't tell her a thing.

Ach. You should have more respect.

EIGHT

The following Thursday, Fig arrived on time to science class, only to discover that his lab report, which he had stayed up late to finish, was not in his book bag. Mrs. Kaminsky paused at his desk to push her glasses up the bridge of her nose and let out a deep sigh, but she said nothing. When the bell rang for study hall the next period, she said, "Well, Mr. Newton, I hope you remember what you wrote late last night, because you have forty-two minutes to rewrite it now."

She didn't believe that he had really done it. That made him mad. But he had no choice. He sat down and began rewriting from memory the list of materials used. About ten minutes into study hall, there was a knock at the open door of Mrs. K.'s classroom, and Gigi poked her head in.

"I don't mean to bother you," Gigi said to Mrs. K., "but I'm Elijah Newton's—oh, Elijah, sweetie. There you are. I found this science paper on the kitchen counter this morning, and since you stayed up so late working on it, I thought it might be important."

Good old Gigi! Fig looked at Mrs. Kaminsky as if to say, "See, I told you so."

Mrs. K. didn't give an inch. She thanked Gigi for the report, then said gruffly to Fig, "Very well. Turn to Chapter 17 and begin your outline." Mrs. K. walked Gigi to the hallway, and for the next several minutes they had a whispered conversation that was—annoyingly—just a bit too quiet for Fig to follow. When the teacher came back into the room, she gave Fig an odd smile, then adjusted her glasses and sat back down to her work.

When Fig arrived home from practice that evening, he was greeted by the inviting aroma of Gigi's famous brisket. Hypnotized by the smell, he followed his nose to the kitchen, where he gave an apron-clad Gigi a big hug. "You're just in time," she declared, holding a second apron out to Fig. "Ready to make latkes?"

Oh no. Fig was famished. He had hoped he was just in time to *eat* dinner, not *make* it.

On the counter sat an enormous pile of potatoes.

Gigi wrapped the apron around his waist and tied it behind his back, then maneuvered Fig toward the mound of potatoes. Like a batting coach with a little leaguer, she wrapped herself around his back and took a hand in each of hers. With her left hand she directed his left hand to a metal grater. In their right hands they took a single potato.

"We don't want your fingertips in the latkes," she explained. "Grip the potato like you grip a baseball bat for a bunt and you won't scrape yourself."

"What do you know about bunting?" Fig asked.

"More than you might think," she answered with a warm smile. "Now pay attention."

Slowly, she guided Fig's hand and together they shredded the potato. When the potato was down to the barest stub, Gigi took it from Fig's hand and finished it off herself, using only her thumb and first two fingers to push the potato against the sharp blades of the shredder.

"Got the idea?" she asked.

Fig nodded.

"Good. Now, you keep your eyes on what you're doing, but listen to me. I'm going to tell you a secret that will win you the hearts of all the ladies."

Fig grinned. "Is that right?"

As he picked up the next potato and began to grate it, she asked, "Now, what is the worst kitchen task besides cleaning the oven?"

"I don't know."

"Guess."

"Doing dishes?"

"Wrong."

"Taking out the garbage?"

"Worse than that!"

"I give up."

"Chopping onions!" Gigi announced.

"You're right," Fig admitted. "That is worse." Even being in the same room with someone who was chopping onions made Fig's eyes sting like mad.

"Chopping onions makes you cry, right?" Gigi said. "No way around it, right?"

Fig nodded and grabbed another potato. Despite his growling stomach, he was enjoying himself.

"Wrong!" Gigi was getting excited. She lowered her voice to a dramatic whisper. "Now, I shall reveal to you the secret."

Fig grabbed another potato. "The secret that's going to 'win the hearts of the ladies'?" he whispered back, mock dramatically.

"Exactly. Now, watch what you're doing there." She took a potato stub from his hand and quickly turned it into hash.

"Gigi?"

"Yes, dear?"

"It might be a while before I plan to cook for any 'ladies.'"

"You're never too young to learn," Gigi said. "So!" Gigi announced, as she often did to change the subject. "So! You didn't even realize I was chopping onions, right next to you."

Fig looked up from the mountain of shredded potatoes. Gigi held aloft a dripping wet cutting board piled high with chopped onion.

"The secret?" he asked.

"Running water!" Gigi declared. "Peel and chop your onions under running water. No more tears."

"And win the hearts of all the ladies."

"Exactly." Gigi reached a hand into the bowl of shredded potatoes. "Very nice. There's hope for you yet."

Fig could not have imagined anything improving on the aroma of the brisket, which was now "resting" on the counter, but the smell of the potato pancakes frying in hot oil made him feel faint from hunger.

"Better call Dad," Gigi said as she placed the first batch of crispy latkes on a plate lined with paper towel.

His father needed no convincing to come to dinner. "I'm surprised the neighbors aren't pounding down the doors, it smells so good in here," he said.

The dining room table was set with Gigi's finest meat dishes. When she had gone back to South Carolina to pack for a longer stay, she had shipped a set of eight meat plates and eight dairy plates from her own collection of fine china, as well as a set of meat silver and dairy silver. When she returned to the Newton home, she had promptly packed up all of their plates, silverware and pots and pans and put them on shelves in the basement. Then she went out and bought a new set—two new sets—of pots and pans.

In the center, where Gigi often placed a vase of fresh flowers, sat a Hanukkah menorah Fig had never seen before. Before they sat down to eat, Gigi handed Fig a half-sheet of paper containing three blessings for the first night of Hanukkah. The words were written in Hebrew letters, but they were also transliterated, so a non-Hebrew reader could at least pronounce the syllables.

"Say the prayers with me—both of you," Gigi commanded. She grinned. "By the end of eight nights you won't need your cheat sheet."

Gigi instructed Fig to light the shamash, the "leader" candle. He then used the shamash to light one additional candle for the first night. The purplish-blue wavy glass of the menorah threw the candlelight in all directions as they said the prayers together.

"Cool," said Fig.

"It's beautiful," his father added. "Where'd you get it, Greta?"

"My great-grandmother," she said proudly. "She brought it with her from Germany when she came to this country."

Gigi gazed at Dad with her calming smile. "Now it belongs to you," she said. "I looked all over the house for yours. If I had known you didn't have a hannukiah to light with this boy, I would have given it to you long ago."

Fig's father looked embarrassed. "Oh, I'm sure we have one somewhere. I put a lot of stuff away when ..." His voice trailed off.

"So! Now you have two," Gigi declared. "Let's eat. Elijah worked hard on these latkes."

Fig's father gave him a surprised look. "You made these?"

"I helped."

"He's a natural, this one," Gigi said, beaming with evident pride.

Fig's dad took a bite. "Hmm, delicious!"

After dinner, Gigi stood up and announced, "I have one small surprise for you, Elijah." She went into the next room, which had been converted from office to guestroom once they saw how weak her chemotherapy treatments made her.

They had never been together at Hanukkah, but each year she sent him two presents. The first was always something Jewish. When he was younger, she had once given him a Noah's Ark play set. Another time she had given him a plush Torah scroll, stuffed like a Teddy bear. Last year he had received *The Jewish Book of Why*, a collection of questions and answers on all facets of Jewish life. The second gift he always liked more. Every year Gigi sent him a big box of books. Most of it was up-to-date young adult stuff, but she always made sure to "challenge" him with a few "classics." At first his dad had made him read the old books, but he had to admit that now he enjoyed them. Gigi was a huge reader, and after her husband had died, she had gotten a part-time job as a children's librarian. In time she had developed a pretty good sense of what kids really liked to read. She never sent him stuff that was too young for him or too girly. He was in the middle of one of last year's books now, *The Adventures of Huckleberry Finn.* Pretty good, with some funny stuff in it.

Gigi returned with a box covered in colorful Hanukkah paper, multicolored dreidels spinning across a blue background.

"No books this year. I know you love to read," she said. "I'm proud of that, and I'll even take a little credit. But since I've been blessed to stay with you two for a while, I've had the opportunity to notice that there is something you love almost as much as soccer."

"Don't tell me you got him pizza for Hanukkah," Fig's father joked.

She handed Fig the box. It was way too light to be books. He wondered what she'd picked out. DVDs?

"Thanks, Gigi," he said, and tore into the package. He hoped they'd be good ones. Now that she was living here, he couldn't exactly return the movies he didn't like.

Fig was stunned.

Inside was an old movie camera.

"It was your grandfather's. He used it to make home movies. It's called a Super 8," Gigi explained.

"I've seen the movie," Fig said.

"What?"

"*Super 8*. There's a movie about some kids who use a Super 8 camera to make a movie."

"Do you like it?"

Fig held the camera up and gazed at it with admiration. "I love it," he said. He gave Gigi a big hug. "Thanks."

"You're welcome, Elijah, sweetie. We'll have to get you some film for it this week."

Fig pointed the camera at his father and made clicking sounds to imitate an old-fashioned film camera rolling. "Say something, Dad," he demanded. His dad was stuffing a final applesauce-soaked latke into his mouth. He covered his mouth with a napkin and swatted at the camera as if it were a pesky mosquito.

Fig dodged his dad's hand and launched into an imitation of a TV newscaster. "We're here with world-famous latke-eating champion Jeffrey Newton," he said. "How many latkes is that tonight, sir?"

"Very impressive, Fig," his dad responded. "I'm sure that's exactly what Gigi had in mind in giving you this camera."

They all laughed. For the moment, Fig forgot all about cancer and Christmas trees, homework and Hebrew classes. For this moment, as the two candles nearly burned themselves out in the menorah, he felt happy to be here with his father and Gigi.

He aimed the camera at Gigi. "Smile," he said.

REMEMBERING NINA
Interview with Jeffrey Allen Newton

You said it would be okay to go back to the question about Mom getting sick.

Sure.

Thank you for being willing to talk about it. I think it's important for the documentary.

You got it, chief.

So, how did you first find out Mom had cancer?

The fall you turned three she got a bad cough, an upper respiratory infection. She took some antibiotics, which seemed to clear things up temporarily, but then it came back, worse than ever. We were concerned that maybe she had pneumonia. When we took her to the doctor for more tests, they discovered the tumor.

Lung cancer. Was she a smoker?

Nope. Just one of those rare, unfair cancers that don't seem to make any sense.

That sucks.

Yes, it does. (*Pause.*) But Nina was a fighter. Unbelievable in a crisis. She took to fighting her cancer like it was a military campaign. She was determined to beat it from the first moment, and the truth is, she never really believed that she wouldn't. I think that's what hurt her most in the end, besides …

What? What is it?

I was going to say, besides the unspeakable sadness of knowing that she wouldn't be around to watch you grow up, the part that was hardest for her to take was accepting the defeat. As weak as she became, as clear as it was to everyone else, it was only at the very, very end—the last few days—that she really, truly let it in that she had lost the fight. She just couldn't believe it. Nina was so stubborn, I'm not sure she'd ever lost anything before, anything she'd really set her mind to.

NINE

Despite the warm glow he'd felt at Hanukkah, Fig woke up a bit depressed on December 25th. He understood—in his head—why they weren't having a tree this year. But Christmastime had always meant a tree, presents.

The smell of pancakes nosed its way under his door, daring him to stay grumpy in the face of such a treat. Gigi must be up. Reluctantly, Fig rolled out of bed, threw on a sweatshirt and padded down the stairs toward the kitchen.

"Hey, chief." His father, clean-shaven, in a bright-blue snowman apron, stood at the stove. He was flipping pancakes. Gigi sat at the table, clinging to a steaming mug like it was a space heater.

The table was set with Gigi's "Desert Rose" dairy plates. He was used to eating off fancy plates—at *Gigi's* house—but wolfing Cocoa Puffs out of a piece of porcelain that was made in the 1700s using a spoon that had been hand-tooled by a Charleston silversmith in the 1840s was taking some getting used to.

Fig sat down and rubbed the remaining slumber from his eyes.

"Good morning, Elijah," Gigi said with a smile. For as long as Fig could remember, it had been "Merry Christmas!" Today it was "Hey, chief" and "Good morning, Elijah." He nodded, determined to resist the serenity drifting toward him on the steam from her tea.

"Morning." He made it a one-syllable word, little more than a grunt.

His father loaded Fig's plate with two pancakes so big they all but covered the pale pink flowers that encircled the edge of the plate, then piled scrambled eggs on top. Without saying a word, Fig got up, grabbed a smaller plate, and scraped the eggs onto it. His dad should know by now he hated to get syrup on his eggs.

They ate in relative silence, but just as Fig was about to attack his last pancake, his father looked at his watch and declared, "Twenty-five minutes."

Fig looked up. His father seemed more than usually chipper. Typical annoying parent thing. Act extra happy to pretend your kid's not miserable. Fig focused on his pancake, unwilling to give his dad the satisfaction of taking the bait and asking, "Twenty-five minutes till what?"

"Christmas morning," his dad said, answering the unasked question. "We're going to church."

Fig squinted hard, as if his father had just begun speaking in a foreign language.

"Oh, Jeff. Don't tease," Gigi scolded. "Elijah, sweetie, your father has found an opportunity for us to volunteer. As a family. We're going to prepare a hot meal for those less fortunate than we."

"Gigi has been doing it every December 25th for years back in Charleston."

He pushed his chair back from the table. "No, thanks. You two have fun."

"Nonsense," his father said. "Go get a shower. We're leaving in twenty minutes."

Fig felt bad, but pretending to be happy at some soup kitchen downtown was just not going to happen. Not today.

"I'm not going, Dad." He stood up from the table. "Tony said I could go over to his house for this brunch thing they do."

"Could you think about somebody other than yourself for five minutes?" his dad started in.

"Give it a rest, will ya?"

Fig got out of there before his dad could launch into some lecture.

The Carrs were still in their church clothes when Fig got there. Tony's sister Erica had on a really pretty, dark-green dress. It might have been the first time in his life Fig had ever seen her not wearing soccer shorts. He felt like a jerk in jeans and a Manchester United jersey.

"Picture time, everybody," Tony's dad announced.

He handed a huge old-fashioned-looking camera to Fig. "You don't mind snapping a couple shots of the gang, do you, Fig?"

Fig looked through the tiny viewfinder and fumbled around with the zoom. The Carrs stood there, arm-in-arm with big smiles on their faces like there was nothing in the world worth worrying about.

Fig took two shots, then Mrs. Carr asked Erica to take a picture of her, Mr. Carr and the two boys. "My adopted son," she joked as she put an arm around each boy and squeezed.

Mrs. Carr had the table set all fancy before church, and now she pulled a piping hot sausage, egg and cheese casserole out of the oven that looked like it should be on a magazine cover or something. "Pour the orange juice, would you, sweetie?" she asked Fig as she headed into the dining room with the casserole.

Fig's stomach hurt. "Sure."

The Hallmark moment continued after brunch, when everyone piled into the family room for *The Polar Express*. Fig could barely sit still. His bell was definitely not tinkling this year. About halfway through, he stood up and whispered a thank you to Mrs. Carr.

"What's wrong, sweetie?" she asked. "You feeling all right?"

"Yeah, I'm good," he said. "Just a little tired, I guess."

Mr. Carr offered him a ride home, but Fig preferred to

walk. On the way, he thought about the day. He could see now that he'd been selfish, and he felt bad about not going with his father and Gigi to volunteer.

TEN

A few weeks later, Fig got home from practice to find Gigi busy in the kitchen.

"How was your day, Elijah, sweetie?"

"Awesome!" said Fig, staring into the fridge. He grabbed a gallon jug of milk. "Coach Green—he's the coach of the Elite team—stopped by our practice for a while, and I was lights out when he was there!"

"Lights out?"

"Everything went great. Everything I did was working," Fig said. "And he noticed, too. He gave me a thumbs-up just as he was gettin' ready to leave!"

"That's wonderful, dear," Gigi said. "You see, I told you a worthy player gets noticed when the time is right."

"And with the next round of tryouts next month, the time is definitely right." Only when Fig grabbed a few cookies from the plate on the counter and sat down at the table next to her did he realize that Gigi wasn't actually cooking. She seemed to be doing some sort of craft.

"What's that?" he asked. The table was covered with

clay pots arranged in a loose semi-circle on some old newspapers Gigi had spread out.

"This evening is Tu B'Shevat, the new year for the trees."

"Tube of what?"

"Tu B'Shevat. It's a holiday," Gigi explained with a smile. "It means the 15th of the month of Shevat, on the Hebrew calendar, and on this day every year we celebrate a new year for the trees."

"Do you make this stuff up?" Fig asked. "Every time I turn around there's another new holiday I've never heard of."

"Oh, there's nothing new about Tu B'Shevat," Gigi answered patiently. "Tu B'Shevat is ancient. It may be bone-chillingly cold here in the snow belt," she continued, "but in Israel, spring has arrived and, with it, cause for celebration. We celebrate the fruits of the land of Israel. There are chopped Israeli dates in those cookies."

"So you're planting a tree—on our kitchen table?"

"I'm planting parsley and a few other herbs. I've done so for years. I start some parsley seeds on Tu B'Shevat, and I've got fresh parsley to adorn my seder plate three months later."

"That's cool."

"Very cool. And you're just in time. There's a bag of potting soil in the trunk of my car that's too heavy for me to carry." She handed him a set of keys with a Bambi key chain Fig had never noticed before.

Fig took the keys and stood up from the table. "I suppose

you're going to tell me Bambi's a symbol of spring renewal, too," he said.

Gigi smiled. "No. Bambi is a symbol that Simcha and Alvin just took the kids to Disney World, and they were nice enough to think of this old grandmother freezing up here in the north."

Gigi had Fig open the bag and pour a mound of potting soil right onto the newspaper-covered tabletop. Then she gave him first choice of painted pots and set him to work. She had a knack for putting Fig to work when he least expected it.

After dinner that evening, Gigi said, "I made a cake— special treat—German chocolate."

Gigi looked at Fig's father in a funny way. He looked stunned.

"German chocolate," he said slowly, hesitantly, as if trying these words together for the first time. "German chocolate."

"I hope you don't mind, Jeff," Gigi said. "I just couldn't resist."

"What's the deal, guys?" Fig asked. "You on another diet, Dad?"

Fig's dad kept his eyes locked with Gigi's. "Today is your mother's birthday—or would have been. Her forty-ninth."

Whoa. That was heavy.

"Hey—that's why you're wearing the Braves cap today," Fig spluttered. "You never wear the Braves."

He finally looked over at Fig. "One day a year," his dad answered, his voice cracking.

"Don't be angry, Jeff."

"No, no, of course not. Of course we should ... mark the occasion ... celebrate her life."

Now it was Fig's turn to be taken by surprise. Celebrate? It was a rare feat to get his dad to talk about Nina at all, and when he did he usually ended up crying, so Fig was surprised to hear the word "celebrate" come out of his mouth.

"Yeah," Dad continued. He shook his head like he was trying to shake himself out of a dream. "So, German chocolate?"

"Nina's all-time favorite," Gigi said.

"From scratch," Fig added.

"All right," his father said, rising to his feet. "Let's get this special cake. I'll scoop ice cream."

"Can't," Fig said authoritatively. "Meat meal."

His dad sat back down at the table. "Meat meal, indeed. Why don't you clear these dishes, Mr. Smart Guy?"

In the kitchen Fig went through drawers until he found a box of birthday candles. He planted four yellow candles in a row on one side of the cake, then an assortment of nine white, pink and blue candles on the other side.

Fig's father and Gigi both laughed when they saw the

makeshift "49" on the cake. His father lit the candles. When Gigi took Fig by the hand, his dad reached out in silence for Fig's other hand. For a moment Fig thought they might end up singing "Happy Birthday to You," but instead the three of them simply stood silently together around the glowing cake.

It was Gigi who broke the silence. "It seems about five minutes ago we were gathered at this very table to celebrate her fortieth. You were such a whirlwind underfoot," Gigi said, letting go of Fig's hand and gesturing under the table and around the room. "Racing from here to there, it made me tired just watching you. But Nina never seemed to notice or mind. 'He's a boy,' I remember her saying. 'Boys bounce.'"

"Please tell me she didn't really say that," Fig demanded. "'Boys bounce'?"

His dad smiled and nodded in agreement with Gigi. Fig felt a sharp, unfamiliar sting in his eyes. He was *not* about to start crying. Sure it was unfair, growing up without a mom around, but he barely remembered Nina. He certainly wasn't going to start crying about missing his mother just because Gigi had made her favorite cake.

"What else did she say?" he asked.

"Nina? What did she say about what?" Dad asked.

"About anything," Fig said. "What kind of things did my mother talk about when she was forty?"

"Oh, she had a lot to say, your mother," Gigi said. "Nina had an opinion about *every*thing."

"But not in a bad way," Dad put in.

"No, of course not," Gigi agreed. "She was a bright, strong woman. She took life very seriously, and when she had something to say, she wasn't afraid to let people know it."

Fig had an idea. "Don't move!" he commanded, bolting from the room. "Stay right where you are and hold that thought." He raced upstairs to his bedroom and grabbed the Super 8 camera. When he returned, he held up the camera. "Let's capture some memories of Nina on her birthday."

"You really shouldn't call your mother by her first name."

"Tell the camera," Fig said.

The presence of the camera seemed to make his dad self-conscious, and he turned away. "We should blow out these candles," he said. "Before they get wax all over the cake."

"Go for it, Dad." Fig pressed the "Record" button. "Make a wish!"

REMEMBERING NINA
Interview with Jeff Newton and Greta Nussbaum
January 15th—Nina's Forty-Ninth Birthday

... Make a wish!

Gigi: Do you want some coffee with your cake, Jeff?
No, no. You've both got to stay right here. I've got questions. You said Nina—my mother—had a lot of opinions about things. What about? Politics? Sports?

Gigi: Hmm. Let's see. When Nina was ten years old she convinced her classmates to save up their glass bottles and newspapers instead of throwing them away, and she corralled a handful of dads to go around once a week and cart the stuff up to a recycling center about twenty miles away. And then for the Bicentennial she waged a campaign against the flying of the Confederate flag in Charleston, wrote her first letter to the editor for that one.

Jeff: That's the Nina Nussbaum I fell in love with. A real firebrand. Our sophomore year, she was one of the leaders of a student takeover of the university president's office—mmm, Greta, this cake is wonderful.

My mother led a riot?

Jeff: It wasn't a riot. It was a demonstration. She felt very strongly about something called apartheid—in South Africa—have you heard of it?

It was like when the minority white government treated the black majority of South Africa like dirt—we learned about it in social studies. But what's taking over the college president's office got to do with being mad about apartheid?

Jeff: Well, she and some other student leaders believed that best way to they could fight apartheid was to pressure the university to divest from South Africa, to take away its investment dollars from any company that did business in South Africa. That's what I loved about Nina. Everybody knew that apartheid was wrong, and lots of people talked about it. But Nina, Nina took action.

Wow! Nina was a radical!

Jeff: You shouldn't call her that.

Gigi: Eat your cake, both of you.

ELEVEN

One morning a few weeks later, as Fig was getting out of the shower, he heard a shriek from Gigi's room. He wrapped himself in a towel and hurried down the hall to her door. He knocked softly. "Gigi? Everything okay?" He put his ear to the door. It sounded like she was crying. "Gigi?"

Gigi's voice was muffled. "My … leg … arm …"

Fig knocked again to let her know he was coming in, then opened the door. "Gigi?"

Gigi lay in a heap next to her bed, her legs twisted under her. She cradled her left arm in her right. She looked like a confused baby bird.

Fig knelt beside her. "What happened?"

"I got up … to go to the bathroom." She spoke in short bursts. "I didn't even … take a step … The next thing … everything hurts."

The fall had knocked the knitted cap Gigi had taken to wearing to bed almost all the way off. The chemotherapy had caused her to lose her hair—she'd been wearing a wig for the last several weeks. Seeing her hairless head was weird. He adjusted the cap back on Gigi's head and said nothing.

"Better get your dad," she said. "My arm." She used her right arm to hold her left arm aloft. "I think it's broken."

Fig looked up at the cuckoo clock Gigi had brought from her house. "Dad had an early meeting," he said. "Maybe Mrs. Carr can drive us to the hospital."

Tony and his mother were due to arrive in ten minutes to drive Fig to school.

Fig tried to help her to her feet. The effort made her cry out in pain.

Gigi's ankle looked pretty messed up. Instead of being where it should, her foot was sort of twisted off to the side and lay limply on the ground. "I'd better call an ambulance," he said.

"No, no," Gigi protested. "Too much fuss." She rocked a couple times and made a strong push with her good leg. Even with Fig's help she couldn't manage to stand.

Fig used a blanket to make a cushion on the floor and helped Gigi to get comfortable right where she was. He gently straightened her left leg and put a pillow beneath her head.

He called 911 first, then he texted Tony to say he wouldn't need a ride to school today. The home phone rang less than a minute later. It was Tony's mom, who had a million questions and who offered to meet them at the hospital.

"We're okay," Fig told her. "Thanks, anyway."

Mrs. Carr said she would call the principal's office to let the school know Fig wouldn't be coming in. He thanked her again, then texted his dad to let him know they were headed to the ER. Fig had just finished tying his sneakers when the ambulance arrived, accompanied by a fire truck. Gigi got increasingly agitated as the paramedics went about their work. "Find my purse, sweetie," she said to Fig. "Make sure my insurance card is in my wallet." Then she directed him to open her top dresser drawer. "At the back of the drawer there is a manila envelope. Hand that to me, please, sweetie." Fig found the envelope. On the front of the envelope, in Gigi's neat script, were the words "Living Will." He wasn't sure what a living will was, but it didn't sound good.

Carefully supporting both her injured limbs, the paramedics loaded Gigi's frail body onto a stretcher and took her out to the ambulance. At the emergency room, Fig followed the paramedics as they wheeled Gigi directly to a curtained examining room. Unlike the three hours he had waited to see a doctor when he sprained his wrist at soccer practice last year, today a nurse immediately began to attend to Gigi, talking with the paramedics and then asking questions.

"I'm so sorry, Greta," Fig's father said—out of breath—when he arrived forty-five minutes later. "I was with patients—I just got your text." He frowned at Fig. "You should have had me *paged*. I could have met the ambulance."

Gigi came to Fig's defense. "We did just fine all by ourselves," she said. "Elijah handled everything perfectly."

Dad blew out a big breath.

"So, what do they say?" he asked.

"The X-ray hasn't come back yet, but it's pretty clear some bones are broken in the ankle and in the upper arm," Gigi said.

"You broke your ankle falling out of bed?"

"She stood up to get out of bed, then fell as soon as she put weight on her foot," Fig explained. "One of the million doctors we've had in here explained that it was probably the ankle bone snapping that caused the fall."

Gigi looked at her son-in-law sympathetically as he digested the information. Fig was pretty sure his father would understand intuitively what the doctors had been hinting at all day: Gigi's dramatically weakened bones most likely meant the one thing they least wanted to hear—the cancer had spread into her bones.

"They want me to stay for a day or two for more tests," she said. "I'm very sorry about all of this."

When visiting hours ended at eight o'clock that evening, Fig was ready to go. Hospitals always gave him the creeps. And he was starved. All he'd eaten all day had come from a vending machine. His dad seemed oblivious to hunger, and despite Gigi urging them to go eat, he dragged his feet until a nurse finally kicked them out at 8:30. They stopped at a drive-thru for burgers and fries. Fig wolfed his down on the way home, and by 9:45, the lights were off in the Newton house.

Fig awoke the next morning to find a note on his bedside table. *Left early to check on Gigi before work. Carrs will take you to school. See you after practice—with takeout.* Dad had added a smiley face to the bottom of the note.

Homework had not even crossed Fig's mind during the day in the hospital, but he managed to muddle through his morning classes without much trouble. That is, until he walked into Mrs. Kaminsky's class and saw the chalkboard: "Chapter Outlines Due Today." Oh, boy.

Mrs. Kaminsky was making some final adjustments at the lab tables in the back of the room, and as she moved to the front of the room, she smiled at Fig.

"Welcome back, Elijah," was all she said. She went from desk to desk collecting outlines from the front of each row, dropped them in a pile on her desk, and began lecturing. Whew! That was close. Fig would have time to explain during the study hall next period.

When the bell rang, he cleared out of the classroom with all the others, stopping at the drinking fountain for a sip of water and hanging out with friends near the lockers, then slipped back into the classroom just before the bell rang for the next period. The whole world didn't need to know he was spending sixth period every day with Mrs. K.

He explained that his absence the day before had been due to Gigi's emergency. Mrs. K. was cool about the missing homework.

"Cancer," she said quietly, taking a seat in a desk next to Fig's. Her face got softer, and although she was looking right at him, she seemed far away. "It's a terrible thing, this cancer. I'm sorry, Elijah."

"What's a living will?" Fig was surprised to hear himself blurt out. He'd been wondering, thought about looking online, but he certainly hadn't planned to ask Mrs. Kaminsky. She explained that a living will was a document that allowed a person to express her wishes about how she would like to be cared for in the case that she was no longer able to express those wishes in person.

"You mean like if she's in a coma or something?"

Mrs. Kaminsky nodded. They were quiet for a moment. Then she said, "You will let me know if there is anything I can do." It wasn't a question. It didn't even sound like an offer. It sounded like an assignment, but in the softer voice she'd been using during their entire conversation. He nodded.

Mrs. Kaminsky stood up. "I'll be in and out setting up the next lab if you have any questions about your report," she said, back in teacher mode. "Work hard."

When practice ended, Fig's dad was nowhere in sight. The Carrs invited Fig to come over for dinner, but he said he'd rather just go home. He usually enjoyed having time to himself at home, but tonight the house felt very empty. Fig tossed his soccer stuff in the breezeway, flipped on the TV on his way to the kitchen, and looked in the freezer for a TV dinner. There were none. Mac and cheese? None of that either. He looked in the fridge. All he could find were chicken breasts and a bunch of fresh fruits and vegetables. He grabbed a bowl and poured himself some Cocoa Puffs. Three helpings later, he put his bowl in the sink and headed for the shower.

Fig tossed his clothes in the hamper in the hallway and was about to walk away when he stopped and looked at the hamper for a moment, as if there was something he was trying to remember. A few moments later, he laughed at himself when he realized he had spaced out staring at the hamper. Gigi insisted on doing the laundry as part of "earning her keep," so it had been a while since he and his father had had to do their own laundry. He grabbed the hamper and headed down to the breezeway to start a load.

Back in his room, he unlocked his art supplies and, sharpening a charcoal pencil, began to sketch. In the first frame, a long rectangle that occupied three-quarters of the top row, Fig found himself drawing a woman in a hospital bed. She looked older and frailer, but there was no mistaking it was Gigi. He was finally starting to get the hang of drawing her face. An IV bag suspended from a pole dripped some sort of medication down a tube and through a needle into her arm. Her eyes were closed and she looked tired but peaceful. In the much smaller next frame two doctors were huddled together, surgical masks covering their mouths. As usual, Fig didn't bother with dialogue. He let the pictures tell the story.

In the next row, Fig's father sat alone in the third frame, on a chair in the hallway. Head bowed, hands folded, waiting. Halfway through a sketch of the doctors conferring with his father, Fig leapt to his feet and went to his closet. He grabbed his camera from the top shelf and turned it on. He walked over to where his sketchbook lay open on his desk, trained the camera on the sketchbook and hit the red record button.

"Thursday, February 6th, 2014," he said, zooming in slowly on his sketch. "Alone in Fig's room." Keeping his hand as steady as possible, he walked very slowly out of his room, down the hall, and downstairs to Gigi's bedroom. He stopped at the bedroom door and held focus on the mezuzah that she had hung on her doorpost.

"Gigi's mezuzah," Fig said aloud. The small box containing a passage from the Torah was the only one in the house. Fig didn't know when Gigi had hung it. She must have brought it back with her from Charleston.

Fig slowly centered the camera on Gigi's door, widening his view at the same time.

"The scene of the crime," he said. He knocked gently. Stupid. Who was going to answer? Then he opened the door and turned on the light.

He scanned the room very slowly with this mechanical

third eye, pausing on Gigi's cuckoo clock, a hatbox, a silver letter opener. On the bedside table, next to a half-full glass of water, Fig's gaze fell on a photograph of his mother on her wedding day. Fig knew this photo well; his dad kept a copy in his office as well. She was beautiful in her wedding gown. On her right stood her father, the grandfather Fig had never known. He was tall, with sharp features. He died of a heart attack almost exactly two years after the picture was taken. He had been a healthy, active man, and the heart attack had come as a complete shock to everyone. In his face Fig saw pride beyond words. To Nina's left stood Gigi, and on her left Aunt Simcha, Nina's older sister. Gigi, not quite as tall as her husband, looked elegant, but her smile seemed a little pinched. Like she was worried about something. Aunt Simcha looked like she always did—distracted. Probably looking over the photographer's shoulder, worrying over one of her own daughters, scurrying around untended by Uncle Alvin.

Closing Gigi's door behind him as quietly as if she were sleeping there, Fig took his camera to the laundry room and, balancing the camera on a box of fabric softener to get the proper angle, recorded himself changing the laundry, this time offering no narration of the scene, then went to bed without even brushing his teeth.

When his father picked him up after practice on Friday, it was the first time they'd seen each other since the day of Gigi's fall. He had been going to the hospital early and then working very late to make up for taking off several hours during each day to be with Gigi.

"Hey, chief." He ruffled Fig's hair. "How was practice?"

"Fine. Is Gigi home?" Fig asked.

His father nodded. "We're going to have to work hard to keep her off her feet. If I know her, she's not going to take kindly to sitting still."

Fig nodded. It would be good to have her back home.

Delicious smells greeted them the moment they arrived home.

"She's cooking?" Fig asked.

"Impossible," Dad said, forcing his Twins cap onto an overburdened hook in the breezeway. "I left her napping on the couch. Greta?"

"Don't worry," she called out from the living room. "I didn't run away."

Fig threw his equipment bag down and headed in to greet her. The only light in the living room came from a big candle holder on the end table, and two more candles burning in the brass candlesticks that Gigi had brought back with her from Charleston. The coffee table, which usually doubled as a footstool when they watched a game or a movie, was set with Gigi's good meat dishes. An enormous challah hid under a cross-stitched cover Fig remembered from visits to South Carolina, and a bottle of wine rested on a wine coaster. The TV, covered with a towel, now served as a pedestal for a tall vase of purplish very long-stemmed flowers. Gigi, though a bit thinner, looked a lot better than when he'd left her in the hospital.

"Bernie and Rachel stopped over just after you left," she explained. "They brought us Shabbos dinner, complete with homemade challah and a kosher Chardonnay they just brought back from California."

"I'm not sure you should have wine, Greta," Dad said.

"Oh hush, Jeff. You worry too much." She grinned. "Elijah, dear, come give Gigi a kiss. Then we'll say the blessings. I haven't had a decent meal in three days."

REMEMBERING NINA
Interview with Greta Nussbaum

You look wonderful, Gigi. How are you feeling today?

I'm happy to be home. The food was awful in the hospital.

Thanks for agreeing to help me with this documentary about my mother. I thought we'd start by looking at some pictures. Okay?

Sure, sweetie.

Tell me about this one.

Oh, where did you ever find that?

It was in a box of my mom's old things.

Yes, well, this here is your mom—do you mind if I point?

Of course not.

This is your mom as a little girl. This here is her friend Rachel Getz. They were best friends all the way through school, till Rachel moved away in maybe seventh or eighth grade. That's the thing with America today— everybody's always on the move. People used to stay in one place.

Where is she now?

Oh, my. I haven't heard from her in years. Let me see, last I heard I think her mother had moved out to California to be closer to Rachel. I suppose with the internet these days you could probably track her down.

How about this one? You brought this one with you to put on your dresser here.

Ah, the beautiful bride. She's gorgeous, isn't she? And so happy. And Papa looks happy. (*Long pause.*) I've sure got a thin-lipped smile there, don't I? Can you keep a secret? Promise not to tell your dad?

We're recording here, Gigi.

I know. I'm teasing with you. Your father knows I love him dearly, and he won't be surprised to hear me say it now. Truth is, I wasn't so happy on your mother's wedding day.

Really? Why not?

Papa and I, we raised our girls to be proud of who they were. We wanted them to marry Jewish men and to raise Jewish children. Simcha, she found herself a nice Jewish boy, a pharmacist. Anyway, I was disappointed that your mother chose to marry a gentile.

But Judaism follows the mom's side, right? I mean, my dad keeps reminding me that because my mother was Jewish, I'm Jewish, no matter what he is.

Sure. And that's what Papa said. He was a pragmatist, a man of the world, like yourself. Me, I had my ideals. And I thought it would be harder for your mother to do right by you in a mixed marriage.

I'll try not to disappoint you, Gigi.

Oh, sweetie, of course not. Of course not. I think you're perfect just the way you are.

Tell that to my dad.

I might just have to do that, come to think about it.

TWELVE

When his alarm went off early Saturday morning, Fig felt like he was going to die. He always woke up excited on game days. Not today. Today his stomach ached, and when he lifted his head, he felt the slight dizziness that usually meant he was about to throw up. His skin felt like a cold noodle, but his pajamas and sheets were soaked with sweat. He turned his alarm clock off, pushed his damp sheet down below his feet and wrapped his wool blanket around himself as tightly as he could. He hugged his pillow to his stomach and curled into a tight ball around it.

The next thing Fig knew, his father was opening the curtains. "RISE AND SHINE, CHIEF!" Dad was screaming. "TIME TO SHOW COACH GREEN HE PICKED THE WRONG MAN." Fig rolled over to avoid the piercing light, and his insides did a flip and then wound themselves into a gnarled lump.

"I feel awful," Fig groaned. "Dad, I can't be sick *today*." It was a terrible morning to wake up sick. Coach Lambert had told the boys at the end of yesterday's practice that

Coach Green, the coach of the Elites, would be attending the game. Fig took a deep breath to gather his strength, then defiantly sat up and swung his legs over the edge of the bed. The room was freezing, and he had to support himself with his hands to stay seated upright.

His father sat next to him on the edge of the bed. "Flu?" he asked, a little quieter.

Fig shrugged. "A little dizzy. I feel like I could puke."

His dad put a warm hand on Fig's forehead. "No fever," he said. "Maybe a nice hot shower will feel good. Clear your sinuses. You sound a little stuffy."

Fig never showered before a game. It was stupid to get cleaned up and then go get all sweaty. But he allowed his dad to help him to his feet and walk him down the hall to the bathroom. The hot pounding of the shower felt good on his stiff neck and shoulders, but even as steam filled the small bathroom, Fig clutched one arm around his chest in an attempt to keep warm. Placing his other hand against the tiled wall of the shower to steady himself, Fig turned his face directly into the stream of steaming water, letting the force of the shower pound his nose and sinuses. Whatever was making him dizzy, he wanted it out of there, even if he had to melt it out.

His dad poked his head in as Fig was dressing himself in slow motion. "All right, chief," he said, chipper again. "Don't want to be late. I'll get the car started."

Fig nodded. The evil in his stomach was still there, but it had stopped squirming around. He grabbed his FC

Barcelona jacket and plodded toward the breezeway to gather his stuff. His father had already packed his soccer bag and taken it to the car—he was being totally cool this morning—and when Fig plopped himself into the passenger's seat, his dad handed him a travel mug with tea and a paper plate with dry toast.

"Feeling any better?" he asked.

Fig shrugged.

"So I started making hotel reservations for our soccer trip."

Fig made himself smile. Nothing was going to make him feel any better this morning, but his dad was sweet to try. Fig didn't touch the toast. He flipped open the lid on the travel mug and held it close to his face.

"FIG NEWTON!!!" Simmy greeted Fig by practically knocking him to the ground with a massive chest bump the moment Fig stepped onto the turf. He was the last to arrive, and everyone was already stretching and juggling to get loose.

"Hit the rock, dude!" Simmy shouted, extending his man-sized fist for a bump. Fig knew that Simmy was pumped about Coach Green being at the game. The Elites' goalie was going to be moving up to the high school next year, and Simmy had a decent shot at his spot.

Fig made a fist and grunted as the other boy pounded his knuckles.

"What's with you?" Tony asked as Fig slumped onto the bench. "You look like crap."

Still moving in slow motion, Fig peeled off his coat. "Thanks, dude," he said, wincing as the chill air hit his bare arms.

Running off to join the guys in a game of keep away with Joey D.'s shin guards, Tony shouted back, "Get warmed up, man."

By the time the team finished their pre-game stretches and warm-up drills, Fig had nearly forgotten about his stomach ache, and when he saw Coach Green walk in and take a seat near the parents' benches, a rush of adrenalin cleared away any lingering sluggishness. Fig studied the other team, clad in the red and white jerseys of the Croatian national team. These guys were always tough. They were a tall, lanky team, and no one controlled the ball better than they did. He needed to step it up today to impress Coach Green. He blasted a final warm-up shot in the direction of the goal, hitting the crossbar, and walked over to where Tony, Simmy and Dieter were horsing around.

"We can beat these guys," Fig said.

They looked at him like he was from Mars.

He hoped that when the starting whistle blew they'd get their heads in the game. "C'mon, guys, let's get serious here. Let's *do* this!"

The Croatian side's center-mid was a good six inches

taller than Fig and must have outweighed him two-to-one. His game was clean but physical. When he banged up against you, you felt it. By the time Coach Lambert pulled Fig for a breather, in the twenty-first minute, he was ready for the break.

The Croatian team scored within thirty seconds of Fig coming out of the game—on a fast break before the subs had gotten their bearings. The score remained locked at 1–0 through the rest of the half, and when the whistle blew for halftime, the guys were visibly exhausted from fruitlessly chasing their opponents' perfect passes up and down the pitch.

Fig sucked at his water bottle, ignoring the shock as the cold liquid splashed into his empty insides. Coach shouted at everyone. "You guys have got to give your keeper a break out there," he yelled. "They're outshooting us four or five to one. Let's take some *shots*." Coach looked over his shoulder at the opposing team, then leaned in toward the boys and lowered his voice as if he had a secret. The guys huddled closer. "Fellows, I got to tell you: every one of those guys expects this match to be a cakewalk," he said, gesturing at the other bench. "We're the underdog here. A tie's a win for us."

Everyone understood what Coach was saying. He didn't have to tell them how awesome it would be to beat these guys. "All right, let's find the back of that net. We keep playing tough defense, and we create opportunities on offense!"

As Fig jumped to his feet for the second half, Coach gave him an encouraging smack on the back and said, "Make something happen out there, Newton."

To start the second half, Fig tapped the ball to Dieter, who flipped it right back. Fig, sensing a crease in the defense, charged head on, dribbling his way to the top of the eighteen-yard box, and blasted a hard shot right at the goalie, who stopped it easily. A second chance came moments later when Raj picked off a rare bad pass and sailed it up over the halfway line to Fig. Again, as soon as he had the ball, he turned on the jets and sped toward the goal. Even a tough bump from his defender, the big kid who had been punishing him all morning, couldn't slow him down. Fig bounced off the bigger boy like a pinball, but never took his eye off the goal, driving straight at it. When the keeper charged toward him to cut off his angle, Fig tried to slip a low shot past him toward the corner. Again his shot was easily stuffed.

"Pass!" Coach yelled as Fig ran past to get back on defense. "Use the space! Use your *team*!"

The next two grueling minutes were spent on the defensive side of the halfway line. The other team slowed the game down, working the ball around in a frustrating game of keep away. As if to rub in how confident they were in their superior ball handling, their keeper came out almost to the center circle and played a sort of point guard as they cycled the ball around, looking for an opening, looking for a mistake. But the defense stayed tough, working together as a fluid, moving wall between the ball and Simmy.

Fig was just beginning to feel desperate when an opportunity presented itself. A Croatian defender misread a pass and started charging forward without having control of the ball, which skidded toward the sideline. Fig practically leapt at the ball and took off in a foot race with his frustrated opponent down the sideline toward the far corner. Out of the corner of his eye, Fig could see Dieter paralleling him down the left side of the field, and he'd been playing with Tony long enough to know that his old friend would be trailing him. Fig made like he was going to take it in all by himself, and then, when he was sure the defender was committed to him, stopped on a dime and, nudged the ball crisply ten feet up and to his left, where Tony suddenly showed, wide open for a shot.

Fig never saw Tony's shot. At the moment he made the pass, the massive center-mid, who had been right on Fig's tail, smashed into him, and the two boys slammed into the turf as one. Before he felt any pain, Fig heard a crunching, ripping sound in his left shoulder, like the combination of a small balloon popping and a car peeling out in gravel. When the pain came a split-second later, Fig felt as if his shoulder had been struck by lightning.

A huddle of faces peered down at him.

"Are you okay?" Coach Lambert asked.

He was breathing in short little gasps. "Tony's … shot?" The pain was worse than anything he'd ever felt, and he fought with everything he had not to cry. "In?"

Coach nodded. It was impossible to smile, but despite

the horrible pain, Fig was pleased. He knew that Tony would tell him about the shot later. Over and over and over.

"Can you …" Fig gasped, "… break … a shoulder?" He allowed his head to fall back on the turf, and he squeezed his eyes shut against the pain.

THIRTEEN

Later that evening, when Fig finally cried, it was not the searing pain of his shoulder separating that brought the tears. It wasn't the dull ache that settled into his shoulder like an arctic freeze during hours of playing one-handed Uno with his dad in the emergency room. Nor was it the take-your-breath-away nightmare of having the orthopedist yank his arm out of his shoulder socket a second time and jam it back where it belonged.

"I'm sorry, but you're going to have to take some significant time off, Elijah," the doctor who set the shoulder explained. "If we can't get this to heal properly, you'll almost certainly need surgery. And we don't want to take any chances."

Fig braced himself. "How long?"

"Three to four weeks is an absolute minimum. But it might be even better if you could stay off the soccer field till next fall," the doctor said.

"Next fall?"

Fig bit his lip and concentrated on a mole just above

the doctor's right eyebrow as the doctor babbled on about "hard pill to swallow" and "better off in the long run." His eyes burned and became blurry. He bit down harder on his lip until the adults stepped out into the hallway, but when the door closed behind them he could hold it in no longer. He sobbed like a little boy whose dog had just been hit by a car.

Fig woke up from a bad dream early the next morning and immediately looked around for something to sketch on. Between constant interruptions and his father's snoring, Fig had tossed and turned all night. It was hard to tell if the fuzzy feeling in his head and achiness all over was from the flu—yesterday morning seemed a lifetime ago—or from the pain medication they had him on. One way or the other, Fig wouldn't recommend a night in hospital for a good time.

His dad, whose red, white, and blue Montreal Expos hat had slipped down over his face, remained oblivious in the chair next to Fig's bed as the morning routine of the hospital wound into full swing, missing temperature checks, a meds distribution, and breakfast: limp scrambled eggs, damp toast, and the tiniest plastic container of apple juice Fig had ever seen.

At 7:40, twenty minutes before visiting hours officially

began, and just as it was starting to sink in that today was going to be a long, unpleasant day, Coach Lambert poked his head around the door, wisps of red hair jutting out from under a Columbus Crew cap. Fig beamed at his coach. Before Coach could open his mouth, Fig put a finger over his lips and nodded toward his father, sprawled in the chair. They'd be able to talk more freely if his father stayed asleep. Coach Lambert stepped into the room, then turned around and put his finger to his lips. Coach Green, the coach of the Elites, followed him into the room.

"Wow!" Fig whispered and wiggled awkwardly to a more upright position.

"Good morning, young man," Coach Green said softly.

"Hey," Fig said. Turning to Coach Lambert he said, "You brought Coach Green." That sounded stupid.

"He brought me," Coach Lambert said. "We play in an old folks' league early Sunday mornings—only time we can get a field. I was going to come by later, but Dave suggested we stop by on the way."

"Had to tell the nurse I was your uncle from Kansas to get her to let us in, but I wanted to see how you were doing," Coach Green said. "That was a nasty spill you took."

Fig nodded.

"You played great out there yesterday," Coach Green continued. "I got to tell you, I didn't think you guys had a chance, but you really stepped it up. You're quite a leader out there."

"Thanks," Fig said quietly.

"I'm counting on you to play for me next year, Fig."

Fig smiled. Should he be happy Coach Green finally noticed him or even more upset that he'd finally caught Coach Green's eye on the day he'd been put out of commission for who knew how long?

Both coaches urged him to take his time to recover fully, reminding him that too many young athletes ruin their long-term chances by coming back too fast and turning an acute injury into a chronic, nagging problem.

"I know what I'm talking about, Fig," Coach Green said. And then, putting his right foot up on the bottom rung of Fig's bed rail, he rolled up his pant leg to reveal pale pink railroad tracks running along either side of his knee. "Tore my ACL in tenth grade. I was too stubborn to listen to the docs or my parents. Came back too fast. I had to have surgery all over again and ended up sitting out my entire junior year."

He rolled his pant leg back down and stood up straight. "Thought I was gonna die."

"How'd you come back?" Fig asked. Everyone knew that Coach Green had played varsity for the University of North Carolina at a time when UNC had one of the best college soccer teams.

"Lot of patience. And a lot of hard work." Coach Green patted Fig's forearm. "Life is long, Fig," he said, as if it all made perfect sense. "You'll get your shot." And with that, the coaches shook Fig's hand and disappeared as quickly as they had appeared.

When his father stretched and opened his eyes a few minutes later, Fig said nothing about the coaches' visit. Anyway, it felt a bit like he had been dreaming, and when his dad stumbled out of the room to track down some coffee, Fig found himself looking around the hospital room for some physical evidence that they had actually been there just moments before.

At 11:30 there was a knock at the door. "Anybody home?" came Gigi's voice from the hallway.

Fig was excited to see his grandmother. "Gigi!"

The door opened and Gigi entered in a hospital wheelchair. "That side, please, Mr. Johnson," she said to the hospital employee she had no doubt sweet-talked into a ride. The man, dressed in burgundy scrubs, wheeled her to the right side of the bed, where Fig's good arm was.

"Thank you kindly, sir. You have a wonderful day."

"How did you get here?" Fig asked.

"I took a cab," she said. "I'm a stubborn old bird, you know. I would have come earlier, but the bookstore didn't open till ten o'clock," she said, as if it was an obvious fact that you couldn't possibly visit a hospital without stopping at a bookstore first. With her only available hand, she held a two-handled bag by one of its handles so Fig could reach inside. Inside was a wrapped package bigger than a book but not heavy enough to be a stack of books.

"This soccer is a new-fangled sport for our family. You come from a long line of baseball people. On both sides. Which I guess makes you a bit of a Muggle."

"Huh?"

"Tell me you've read *Harry Potter*, Elijah, sweetie. As a soccer player in a baseball family, you're a Muggle in a family of wizards."

It hurt a little when Fig laughed.

"Here! Open it. I think you'll like it anyway."

Working together with one good hand each, Fig and Gigi managed to dump the package gently out of the bag, and Fig tore the paper off a box set of DVDs entitled *Baseball: A Film by Ken Burns*.

"It's a documentary," Gigi explained. "Do you know what a documentary is?"

Fig nodded, less than enthusiastic. "It's like a movie about something real," he said. "We watch them in social studies sometimes."

"This one's better than those," said Gigi. "Trust me." Then she noticed the TV in Fig's room. "So!" she said sharply. "Don't take my word for it. If we can get someone to tell us how to work this machine, you can see for yourself."

Fig pressed the red call button for an aide, and minutes later they were watching Baltimore's Brooks Robinson single-handedly take the 1970 World Series from the Cincinnati Reds.

"I've always appreciated the hopefulness that comes with the springtime, the beginning of a new season," Gigi said. "I thought a little winter baseball might take your mind off things."

Fig just smiled and nodded. Nothing was going to take his mind off the pain in his shoulder, but she was nice to try.

His father returned to the room just as the lunch cart came in. "Greta? How did you get here?"

"I jogged." Gigi winked at Fig. "Can't you see I'm lathered in perspiration?"

His dad evidently decided to let the matter go. They watched Fig eat his lunch, then Fig's dad took Gigi home to get some rest. Fig asked them to pop in "Inning 6," the DVD from the *Baseball* series that included the Forties, the last time the Cleveland Indians won the World Series. He watched for a while, but nodded off to sleep before the episode got to the part about the Indians winning. When he woke up, the screen was filled with fuzz. Fig laughed at the thought of himself as a sort of baseball Rip Van Winkle, an old man who'd waited his whole life to see his team win the Series, only to fall asleep just before the big moment.

A couple of napkins on the sliding table perched over his lap caught his eye, and Fig's fingers itched to do some sketching. Trying to ignore the pain in his shoulder, he leaned over to reach for an ink pen on the bedside table, but when he tried to sketch, the pen cut through the napkin. Fig adjusted his approach, taking light, feathery strokes, and within minutes his mother's face appeared on the napkin in front of him. She appeared the way she almost always did—wedding dress, big smile—the image from the photo in his dad's office, currently Gigi's bedroom. Looking over his sketch, Fig realized that even her arms were in the same position in his sketch and in the photo. In fact, anytime he thought of her, that's how she looked: wedding dress and big smile. There was something comforting about that big smile, but Fig wondered what her face looked like when she was sad. Or when she pulled someone's tooth. Or when her baby—Fig as a baby—wouldn't stop crying. Or when she watched Henry Aaron hit that record-breaking home run.

On a second napkin Fig started another sketch. He started with the face—same face, same smile. He wasn't ready to mess with the face. But this time he put her in a Braves cap. He replaced the wedding dress with an untucked jersey and a pair of jeans. In her hand, which he moved from its ordinary location, he placed a soda cup. Would she have eaten a hot dog at a ball game? Popcorn? Did they even have cotton candy back then? There were so many things he didn't know.

Studying the pair of sketches he'd made, Fig wrote in all caps "WHAT WERE YOU LIKE?"

Just then, his father bounded into the room with a duffel bag. He was clean shaven and wearing fresh clothes and a different ball cap, a 1970s Pirates cap, mustard yellow with a black "P."

"They're setting you free!"

"Sounds good," Fig said, crumpling his sketches into a

tight ball. "I'd be happy if I never saw the inside of this place ever again."

As his father helped Fig get dressed to go home, Fig asked, "So who did my mother root for in the '95 series—Atlanta or Cleveland?"

Dad looked up, surprised. "Whoa—where did that come from?"

Fig gestured toward the box of DVDs from Gigi.

"Right," said his father, nodding. "Well, being from the South, she supported the Atlanta Braves, of course. Made it hard to watch the games together. Especially Game 6, the deciding game." He chuckled. "But she was gracious about it, as she was in all things. Took me out for wings and beers afterward. To help me 'drown my sorrows,' she said."

"Real beers?"

"We were adults, you know. It is legal for an adult to drink beer."

Fig was confused. "But you don't drink."

"Yeah, well, there was a time."

REMEMBERING NINA
Interview with Edith "Edie" Goldfarb

I'm sitting here with Mrs. Edith Goldfarb, Dr. Nina Nussbaum's office manager and herself a former patient. Thank you for agreeing to talk with me, Mrs. Goldfarb.

Certainly, Elijah. But you have to call me Edie. Everyone does.

Then you have to call me Fig—everyone does.

Your mother didn't. She called you Elijah. That, and "Sunshine."

"Sunshine?"

Yes, sir. And of course sometimes she'd use your full name. She had a picture of you in every room in the office, and sometimes, in the middle of a check-up, she'd just look over at you and smile and say, "Elijah Samuel Newton." You had her wrapped around your little finger.

Really?

I wouldn't lie to you.

Wow. (Pause.) Well, as I told you, I'm making a documentary about Dr. Nussbaum's life, and in order to have a complete picture, I need to know what she was like professionally. What was she like as a dentist?

Oh, Dr. Nina was wonderful. Very professional, quite demanding—ran the office like clockwork—but all the girls in the office, we loved her. The man who bought the practice is a very fine dentist, a good man, but it's just not the same. Dr. Nina was something special.

That's what you called her—Dr. Nina?

That's right. All us girls did.

You were also a patient, right?

She had the most wonderful bedside manner, if you will. Not everyone likes to have someone jabbing around in their mouth, but Dr. Nina was very soothing.

Was that weird, having your boss check for cavities?

She was my dentist before she was my boss. But only for about an hour. My husband lost his job, see, so we were without insurance, and I got the most awful toothache. I started calling dentists in the area, and she was the first one who would agree to take me. She was brand new in practice—answered the phone herself, actually. Said it didn't matter how long it took me to pay. "We can't have you walking around with a toothache, can we?" That's what she says. So I say, "And we can't have the good doctor answering her own phone, now, can we?" So that afternoon I had myself a new dentist and a new job.

FOURTEEN

For the entire first week after the injury, just breathing caused pain in his shoulder and across his back, so Fig needed to be very careful about what he did. The doctor had told him it was important to stay active but to take it easy, so Fig started with walking. After just a week he was able to start kicking a ball against the basement wall and jogging outside. It hurt—not so much while he was drilling or jogging, but later, especially when he got into bed at night.

The night before he went back to school, Tony came over. Fig showed him the *Baseball* DVDs. Tony wanted to watch the Babe Ruth parts. While Tony watched, Fig got up to get them something to drink. When he came back he said, "I've been thinking about making a video about the team, sort of a documentary."

"Dude, you know what you should call it?" Tony said. "*Soccu*mentary!"

"Soccumentary?"

"You know, like, *soc*cer and documentary." He spoke slowly and loudly, as though Fig were unlikely to understand.

"That's corny."

"Yup," Tony agreed with a grin. "But it's a cool idea. You should do it."

At lunch on his first day back, Fig headed for the weight room. A few machines he could do with legs only, but he was determined not to lose too much conditioning while his stupid shoulder healed. He also wasted no time in getting back to practice. Instead of soccer equipment, he packed his Super 8 camera and a sketchbook in his gym bag.

Coach seemed pleasantly surprised to see him. "Fig! How's the shoulder, young man?"

"It's all right. I have a question."

"Shoot."

From watching the baseball movie, Fig had decided that he would intersperse soccer action with interviews of the coach and key players. He wasn't sure how he was going to do that yet. To make things easier, he decided to start by focusing on one individual at a time, and who better to start with than Coach Lambert?

"Do you mind if I take some film footage during practice? I was hoping to make a short movie about the team." He felt weird telling Coach he was making a "documentary."

Coach had no sooner said "Sure" than Fig started digging into his gym bag with his free arm. "Do you have a few minutes right now? I'd like to ask you a few questions for my movie."

"Sure, Fig." He looked at his watch. "I got five minutes."

Fig was relieved. "Thanks, Coach." He set the camera on his lap, worked his hand into the strap around the camera, and flipped it on with his thumb. He trained the camera on this man he admired so much. Since he was sitting only a few feet from Coach, Fig had to zoom out to make his coach fit onto the camera's view screen. Fig noticed a touch of grey hair at the temples, and looking closely at his coach's face, he could see that his skin was run through with a light web of wrinkles. Holding the camera as still as possible, Fig said, "Please state your full name." Coach Lambert took off his black and yellow Columbus Crew cap and made a show of fixing his hair just so. He was bald on top, with straws of straight red hair that hung like a curtain around the sides and back. Placing his cap back on his head, all important, he announced, "James William Lambert, Jr."

True to his word, after five minutes of questions, Coach waved off the camera and stepped toward the gym, where the guys were warming up. "Gotta get started. Stick around and shoot all you want."

That afternoon and during the team's next match, Fig kept his camera trained on Coach Lambert. He took footage of Coach running drills in practice. He caught Coach yelling at the referee and high-fiving players during the game, and he captured a fiery halftime pep talk.

Throughout the following week, Fig turned his attention to the players. It was frustrating not to be on the field playing, but watching the action so closely was at least interesting. That Saturday they faced Cleveland Strikers FC, a team that always beat them. In fact, sometimes Fig and his teammates came away from a match with the Strikers feeling as though they'd been on the losing end of a game of keep away. Everyone knew that Strikers FC's players had very good foot skills, and they were very disciplined passers. Training his camera on one player after another during the match, Fig was able to see some things he'd never noticed when he was so focused on what he himself was doing.

He knew that most guys his age didn't yet have the skills not to have to look down at their feet at least a little when handling the ball, but as the match went on, Fig noticed that the best passers were the ones who never seemed to need to look down, instead keeping their eyes open for just the right opportunity to hit an open teammate with a pass and keep the ball moving down the field.

Fig shut the camera off and just watched for a while. Coach Lambert always reminded them that because casual fans usually just followed the ball, they tended to miss a lot of little things that can make a difference in the game. Choosing a single player to focus on whether he had the ball or not forced Fig to notice some of these "little things," like positioning, getting open, reading the play that was developing, and communicating with teammates. Fig felt he could add something to Coach's advice: "Don't be fooled into assuming the best player on the field is the guy with the fanciest footwork or the guy who takes the most shots." It was quite possible that the best player on the field wasn't even a guy who drew the attention of the fans at all. When he felt pretty sure he had determined who the best player on the field was—number 9, a well-built but not super-tall mid-fielder who never seemed to look anywhere in particular, but rather to be scanning the field at all times, Fig trained his camera on that kid. Over the final twenty minutes of the match, Strikers FC scored three more goals, and #9 was central to the development of all three. He got two assists, including one by driving hard then passing at the last possible moment outside to set up a beautiful service back into the box. And on one goal he had been crucial to the play without even touching the ball, but by seeing an opening and calling his teammates' attention to it.

When Fig was feeling up to it, Tony came over and the two friends worked on some passing drills. Fig knew he was going to have to ease back into playing time, and until he was back to a hundred percent, he figured he was going to be able to contribute more by supporting an attack than by leading one. Fig focused intently on passing and receiving the ball without looking down at his feet. And he and Tony worked obsessively on give-and-go till they got to the point they were practically reading each other's minds, Fig hitting Tony in perfect stride over and over again.

After a few weeks of filming practices and games, Fig was beginning to wonder how to turn all these hours of video footage into the smooth style of a real documentary. He'd been studying Ken Burns' *Baseball* religiously. It was time to figure out how to splice it together, how to balance action shots with interview clips. He wondered if it might even be possible to get voiceovers from interviews right in with the action footage. It was going to take a lot of work, but he was determined that this was going to be a documentary worth watching.

During study hall in Mrs. Kaminsky's room one afternoon, Fig chewed on this problem the same way he worked out any problem—by sketching. He was able easily to select from memory exact moments he wanted to include in his documentary. The first several frames showed Coach Lambert's actions on the sidelines during the game: shouting, pointing, punching a fist into the air to celebrate a goal. The next frame featured a close-up of Coach at his desk, cap in hand, patting down his hair. Then came the coach being interviewed and featured the caption "James William Lambert, Jr.—Midgets' Coach." The next several cells alternated between images of Coach Lambert at his desk and a variety of images of soccer action.

"Funny—that graph looks a lot like a soccer field." Mrs. Kaminsky's voice over his right shoulder caught Fig off guard. The last time he'd checked, she'd been safely absorbed in her lab equipment in the back of the room. He quickly slammed his sketchbook shut.

"Sorry, Mrs. K. My mind wanders sometimes."

"I've had occasion to notice," she said, with a hint of a smile—more in her eyes than on her lips. "But today it looks to me like your mind has been very focused. Let me see what we have here." She reached for the sketchbook.

Fig was embarrassed. "Really, it's okay." With his one good hand he tried to work his sketchbook into his overstuffed backpack.

"Show me. Please. I'd like to see your work." Mrs. Kaminsky's voice was softer now, and when she referred to his sketches as his "work," there was no trace of sarcasm in her voice. He opened the sketchbook and handed it to her. With the exception of a few nods of the head, her face revealed nothing as she studied the pages.

"It's just a sketch," Fig said, finally unable to resist defending his drawings in the face of her silence.

"These drawings are very good." Mrs. Kaminsky did not look up from the notebook. "It is a movie you've seen?"

"Sort of."

Now she looked up at Fig, but said nothing. She was waiting for him to say more. Mrs. Kaminsky was not in the habit of letting students off the hook with evasive answers to direct questions.

"It's sort of a movie I've been working on." He blew out an anxious breath. "Sort of a documentary."

Mrs. Kaminsky raised an eyebrow and waited again.

Worn down by her persistence, Fig spilled everything. His love for movies, Gigi's gift of his grandfather's camera, the baseball documentary, and his decision to make a short documentary about his soccer team. He explained his plan to splice together interviews with action shots.

"And I'm planning to use background music—a soundtrack," he said at last. "Now I just need to figure out how to do it. I've messed around a bunch with video editing before, but Super 8 is different."

Mrs. Kaminsky seemed to be looking at his sketches and staring into space at the same time. Then she straightened up and clapped her hands together the way she always did when she was ready to move on.

Fig was disappointed. He had not planned to tell Mrs. K. all that stuff about his movie, but now that he had, he was hoping for a response of some sort. He leaned his sketchbook against his book bag on the floor and was about to ask her a question about the bar graph he was supposed to be making when she announced, "Come with me." She pushed her glasses up the bridge of her nose. "Quickly— we only have a few minutes." There was an excitement in her voice that she usually reserved for lectures on DNA or osmosis, and she was moving rapidly toward the door of the classroom.

"Bring your drawings!" she shouted over her shoulder as she cruised out the door.

Fig hurried to catch up with her and had to walk fast to keep up as they headed down the long corridor of the Science Wing.

"Where are we going?" he asked as they turned into the main hallway of the middle school.

"MSBS," came the response. Of course! "MSBS" stood for Middle School Broadcast System, the two-minute student-produced video "news" segment shown in homeroom every morning, along with the principal's announcements over the loudspeaker.

Mrs. Kaminsky raced down two flights of stairs and through a door marked "Audio-Visual, K. Moffett." Behind that door lay a cramped jungle of oversized television sets strapped precariously atop metal carts like captured dinosaurs, filmstrip and overhead projectors, and large beige cassette tape recorders.

"Mr. Moffett!" Mrs. Kaminsky practically sang the name.

There was some rustling from around the corner in the small corridor of a room, the tinkling of bells, and a pair of adorable West Highland White Terriers appeared from around the corner.

"Which one's Mr. Moffett?" Fig joked, leaning down to pet the Westies.

"That'd be me, young man," said one of the deepest voices Fig had ever heard. Fig looked up and saw a thin man of medium height—how did this dude ever get such a deep voice?—with a white mustache and a tweed cap on his head. "And who might you be?"

"This is Elijah Newton," Mrs. Kaminsky answered for him. "He's got a project you might be interested to know about, and I wondered if you'd be able to help him."

"Well, thank you kindly, Nadia," the man said with a slight bow. "Never enough work, you know." Mrs. K. was bound to miss the sarcasm. He turned to Fig. "What's itching you, young man?"

While the Westies competed to lick Fig's fingers, he quickly told Mr. Moffett about his project and what he needed.

"Super 8 film!" Mr. Moffett boomed as if he were announcing an exciting new technology. "Got just the thing. Follow me." Mrs. Kaminsky left Fig with Mr. Moffett and his dogs, and Fig followed his new guide around the corner of the cramped equipment room to a small area that was set up like an office. In one corner a set of small, mismatched oblong tables had been set up in an L-shape, and atop it sat a combo of five computers and television monitors shackled together by a tangle of electrical wires. Though slightly more modern than the equipment which greeted Fig upon entering the room, everything on these tables had seen better days.

"This, my young friend, is where the magic happens," Mr. Moffett intoned. And for the next twenty minutes he proceeded to demonstrate to Fig the video editing process he was engaged in for the next edition of the MSBS news, explaining how students took more than twenty minutes of footage on three different cameras for a typical two-minute segment, and showing off some of the techniques through which he coaxed this collection of machines to create the smooth, continuous flow of images viewers expect from TV. It was awesome!

Fig hardly noticed when the bell rang to signal the

change of classes, and when Mr. Moffett finally wrote him a late pass and invited him to stop by after school to "get down to business," Fig was thrilled.

Skipping soccer practice after school, Fig worked side-by-side with Mr. Moffett in the crowded A-V room. Editing was painstaking but fun, and three hours passed quickly. The result was a four-and-a-half-minute segment that was more like what Fig had pictured in his mind than he could ever have hoped to achieve on his own. They were even able to get voiceovers from interviews into some of the action scenes. All that was missing was background music. They agreed that Fig would select some music to add in the next day.

Fig thanked Mr. Moffett for his help, then asked if he could use the phone. "I think I left my cell phone at home this morning."

"Where are you, Elijah, sweetie?" Gigi asked when he called home. "Your father called from the soccer field thirty minutes ago worried sick. I'm not sure I've ever heard him this upset."

REMEMBERING NINA
Interview with Greta Nussbaum

So why do you think it was so important to my mother that I have a bar mitzvah?

One does not *have* a bar mitzvah, Elijah. One *becomes* a bar mitzvah, a son of the mitzvot, the commandments. Party or no party, becoming a bar mitzvah happens to every Jewish boy at age thirteen. It's just who you are.

FIFTEEN

Dad was still steaming when he arrived at school to pick up Fig, and he ranted the entire way home about responsibility. He also grounded Fig for the weekend, including Saturday morning's soccer game. "Anyway, I've got a quick work trip out of town," Dad said. "I need you to stay and take care of Gigi," he said.

"But Gigi spends Shabbat with her friends," he replied.

"Not this weekend, she doesn't, chief," Dad said. "This weekend she's right here. And so are you."

Fig wasn't sure whether Gigi was staying home this weekend to be with him, or if he'd been grounded primarily because his father wanted someone to be home with Gigi. Either way, Fig came directly home from school on Friday, and he and Gigi enjoyed a delicious Shabbat dinner together.

The glow of the candlelight, the sound of Gigi's voice singing the prayers, perhaps even the taste of wine she had put into his glass—all had a softening effect on Fig. Here, alone with Gigi, a simple yet beautiful meal on the table, he felt part of something bigger than himself. And he could see how happy it made her to be here with him, even though he knew she was disappointed not to be going to services in the morning.

"We could walk to my synagogue, you know," he said. "They have a service at 10 o'clock in the morning."

Gigi looked up. "They do?"

Fig nodded, gnawing on an oversized piece of homemade challah. "Dad made me miss a game once when the whole bar mitzvah class had to go together."

She observed him for a long moment. "How far is it?"

Fig shrugged. "I don't know. Tony and I jog right by it, so it can't be that far. Maybe two, three miles."

Gigi looked down, the light in her eyes dimmed. "Oh, sweetie, my ankle's doing a lot better, but I couldn't make it two or three miles yet."

"I'll push you," Fig said, warming to the idea. "I know you hate to use that wheelchair Dad got you, but maybe you'll make an exception tomorrow." Fig wasn't a huge fan of sitting through services, so he wasn't sure why he was suddenly so gung-ho about pushing Gigi all the way to temple.

"Elijah, sweetie, you have one good arm."

"We'll be fine. We'll be a team." As if to punctuate his point, he reached for the challah with his available right hand and Gigi held down the loaf with her free hand while he tore off a piece. He was just about to take a bite when he stopped and offered it to Gigi.

"Thank you," she said, accepting the bread. She held the loaf again and Fig tore a piece for himself. Gigi gazed at him while he chewed. The light was back in her eyes.

"Do you really think you could do it?" she asked.

"*We*, you mean?" Fig grinned. "Piece of cake."

The next morning came sooner than Fig would have liked. When his alarm went off, he plodded down to the basement to loosen up and do some passing drills. When he stepped out of the shower an hour later, he heard Gigi singing in the kitchen, and when he came down for breakfast she was elegantly dressed in a plum-colored dress with matching shoes. A shawl hung over the chair. On her plate sat a half-eaten piece of coffee cake and two thin slices of cheese. She sipped a small glass of orange juice.

Fig helped himself to a large slice of coffee cake.

"Are you sure you're up for this, Elijah?"

He smiled. "No pulling out now, Gigi. I don't shower before noon on weekends without a good reason, you know."

She looked over at the clock. "Well, then, we'd better get going. It might take longer than we think," she said. Fig zipped over to the breezeway. He had a surprise for Gigi. Opening the door to the garage with a flourish, Fig said, "Ta da! Check this out!" In the spot where his dad's car was usually parked sat the wheelchair he had borrowed for Gigi after her fall. Dangling from one side of the wheelchair was a crutch, as if overnight the chair had sprouted a single, misshapen wing. Fig had attached it to the chair's left handle with about a roll of silvery duct tape.

Gigi looked puzzled.

"Your ride," Fig announced. "Watch." Slowly, using only his free right hand, Fig undid his belt buckle, pulled the belt back through the loops one by one until it almost fell free, and then fed the belt through the opening and around the hand grip of the crutch and back, one by one, through his belt loops.

"I thought of this last night," Fig declared. "Let's test it out."

Gigi took a seat, and they worked together, one hand each, to connect the wheelchair's seat belt across her lap.

"Here goes!" Fig said, leaning his weight forward into the back of the wheelchair. Sure enough, his belt nudged the crutch forward, which in turn pushed the left handle of the chair. He grasped the right handle of the chair and took a few steps.

"Perfect!" he said, pleased to see his contraption was going to work.

Gigi smiled. "Perfect," she agreed.

They headed out the garage door and down the driveway for their first walk together since the first week of Gigi's visit last fall. The evening she had told him about the cancer. A lifetime ago.

The left turn onto the sidewalk was easy to maneuver. Fig simply planted his left foot like a basketball player going into a pivot and pushed forward with his right hand, his body weight naturally propelling the wheelchair into a left turn.

The sidewalk was slick from overnight rain, but as they sailed smoothly down the sidewalk, the sun shone brightly in the eastern sky.

As they approached the end of their street, the sidewalk stopped short of connecting with the main road. To head toward the synagogue, they would need to cross the main street, then turn right onto the sidewalk, which only ran on the north side of the road.

A maroon Subaru pulled up next to them and Tony's father rolled down the passenger window. "Good morning, folks," he called out. "Give you a lift somewhere?"

Fig looked at Gigi.

"Thank you kindly all the same," she responded with a smile. Always a smile. "But I've got a fine ride already."

Mr. Carr gave them a wave and made the right turn out of the neighborhood. Fig maneuvered the crossing easily, and soon they too were cruising east on the road which would take them the remaining two-plus miles to the synagogue. Out here, the sidewalk was older and less smooth, and Fig worried that the bumpy ride might be hard on Gigi's healing fractures.

"You doing all right, Gigi?" he asked.

"I think so. How about you?"

"I'm doing great," he replied. "It's an adventure."

Two hundred feet later, the adventure intensified, as they perched atop the only hill on their route, a relatively steep down-then-up that would take them under a freeway overpass. Instead of pushing, the trick now was to keep the wheelchair from going too fast. As gravity pulled the vehicle and its rider down the hill, the wheelchair kept tugging to the left. With her one available hand, Gigi gripped the arm of her wheelchair.

"I'm not going to let you fall out," Fig said.

"You focus on steering this thing," Gigi said. "I'll make sure I don't fall out."

Fig had an idea. He brought the wheelchair to a stop and, reaching around front, engaged the brake on the left wheel of the chair. In this way, slowly, his right hand steadying the right side of the wheelchair, the left side slowed by the mechanism of the brake, they inched their way to the bottom of the slope.

Getting up was easier. Fig loosened the brake, and making a wall of his right shoulder and his chest, used his whole body to drive the chair up the hill. He broke into a jog to generate some momentum, the wheelchair bounced happily along, and Gigi, clutching her bag more tightly against her, let out a laugh.

"I'm glad *you're* having fun," Fig grunted, and in a minute they had made it to the top of the slope. Fig maintained his jog to take advantage of the green light across what would be the busiest intersection on their route, until the blare of a horn stopped him short as a dark-green SUV screeched to a stop in the middle of a right turn on red.

Fig glared at the teenage driver behind the wheel. "What the heck?" he shouted. "She didn't even stop at the light before turning!"

As the embarrassed driver motioned for them to cross in front of her, Gigi let out a deep breath and recommended that they get out of the road before the light changed.

Safely on the other side, Fig stopped to catch his breath. Gigi was practically grinning, seemingly unmoved by the near accident. "Oh, sweetie, you're soaked," she said. "You'll expire before we're halfway there."

Fig laughed. Gigi even had fancy words for croaking. "I won't *expire*. Trust me. That's the only hill between here and the temple."

It may have been the only incline that would fit a strict definition of a hill, but it didn't take Fig long to realize that the slope of a road is a lot less noticeable when you're riding in a car than when you're pushing a wheelchair with one hand.

He looked at his watch. They were making good time. He adjusted the belt arrangement and nudged the wheelchair into motion again. The next ten minutes went smoothly. With the exception of a few patches where rough sidewalk or deep cracks required Fig to slow down or to maneuver gently, they were able to settle into a steady rhythm.

"Uh-oh!" Gigi said, pointing.

About three hundred feet ahead, blocked off by a

wall of bright orange construction barrels connected by a whole bunch of plastic webbing of the same color, a hulking yellow backhoe was digging up a lengthy section of sidewalk.

Fig looked across the street. Still no sidewalk. What kind of town puts a sidewalk on only one side of its busiest street? A worker in a bright orange vest was marching toward them as they inched closer to the construction site. Fig, whose mood was taking a turn for the worse, was prepared to bark back if this guy started yelling at them about "can't they see this is a construction site".

"Sidewalk's only blocked for about two hundred feet," the man shouted in greeting. "Shouldn't be too hard to get past. Let me give you a hand."

One of the guy's eyes seemed unwilling to go where the man was trying to look, and Fig had trouble figuring out which eye was looking at him, so he focused on the man's mouth when he spoke.

"Thank you kindly, sir," Gigi answered. "That would be most helpful."

The grass, soaked by the overnight rain, was not an option. Even with a light passenger, the wheelchair's large back wheels bit deeply into the turf. They opted for the street.

"That's quite a contraption you've rigged up there," the man said to Fig as he helped lift Gigi over the curb onto the street, where, rather than help Fig push, he decided to walk ahead of the pair and nudge oncoming traffic toward the center line.

As they reached the far edge of the construction site, their guide stopped and, continuing to face oncoming traffic, shouted over his shoulder, "Can you get her back up on the sidewalk yourself?"

"The ride is a lot smoother out here, actually," Gigi announced matter-of-factly.

"Gigi, it's the middle of a busy street," Fig said. "It's not safe."

"It's not the middle," Gigi retorted, "And all morning we've been watching cyclists who seem very comfortable on the edge of traffic."

Now it was the construction worker's turn. "I can't advise it, ma'am," he said, his body still turned toward the oncoming traffic. "And I'm sorry, but I can't go with you any further."

"We'll be fine," Gigi said confidently. "Thank you again for your kindness."

The man nodded to Gigi, then looked at Fig. "All right, but be careful. And stay on this side. It's safer to walk with the traffic coming at you than to have cars sneaking up from behind. You got to watch these cars like a hawk." And with that, he crossed his arms over his belly, pulled off his bright orange vest and handed it to Gigi. Together they pulled the vest over the bag she held on her lap, as if this was something they did all the time.

"Why thank you, Mr. Nahor," Gigi said, reading off the nametag on the vest. "You've been most kind." Then, emboldened by her increased visibility, Gigi playfully shouted, "Onward, young man!" Rolling his eyes, Fig dutifully nudged his chariot forward to face the challenges ahead.

He didn't have to wait long for the next one. With no more warning than a brief rustling of leaves, it began to rain.

"Oh, no," Fig groaned. "What next?"

"Not to worry," Gigi said, digging into the bag on her lap. "I brought ponchos."

"Of course you did!"

Thirty-three minutes later, shoes and pant legs soaked through, they arrived at the synagogue.

"I'm sorry, Gigi," Fig said in frustration, as he nosed the wheelchair across the street. "It was a terrible idea to do this. You must be freezing, and now we're stuck here with no way to get home."

"Nonsense," Gigi said. "It's been a brilliant adventure. Now let's get inside, where it's dry."

Inside, Fig headed straight for the coat room. He undid his belt buckle and freed himself from the wheelchair, then helped Gigi out of her poncho and hung it to dry. As he was wrestling to get the bright orange wet plastic over his own head, he heard an unfamiliar voice say, "Wow! Looks like the two of you floated here."

Yanking the poncho off, Fig saw a tall, slender girl with

wavy, shoulder-length dark hair and a delightful smile. Ninth, maybe tenth grader.

"I'm Rebecca," the girl said. "I help out with Sunday school for the little guys. I'll bet if we look in the lost and found we could find you two something dry to warm up in." And with that, Rebecca turned and started down the hall. They followed their new guide to the main office, and a quick search produced identical pairs of navy and gold Crestmount High sweat pants.

"I don't wear Crestmount colors," Fig said.

"And I don't *ordinarily* wear sweatpants," Gigi admonished. "But today's not an ordinary day, Elijah, sweetie. Go change out of those wet pants."

From behind Gigi, Rebecca gave Fig a teasing look, grinning and raising her eyebrows as if to say "So, there!" And when she did, he noticed that her eyes were—grey. Actually grey. Everybody always told him his mother's eyes were grey, but he had never quite believed it, because he'd never seen grey eyes in real life.

"What color are your eyes?" he asked Rebecca.

She looked at him as if he were a bug. "Nice to meet you, too, Elijah."

"Fig. They call me Fig," he explained.

"Who's they?" she replied, evidently determined to give him a hard time. "Who calls you Fig?"

"Everybody but his grandmother, that's who," Gigi said. "Young lady, if I could ask one more kindness, I think I'm going to need a little help with these sweatpants."

Rebecca and Gigi headed down the hall toward the ladies' room as though they'd known one another for years. Turning the sweatpants inside out to hide the rival school's logo, Fig changed quickly and waited for Gigi to emerge. The wet hem of Gigi's dress came down to her ankles, but it was funny nonetheless to see the navy sweatpants covering the gap between the hem of her dress and the elegant shoes she was now wearing.

"I offered to make some tea to warm you two up," Rebecca announced, all welcome committee. "But your grandmother insists we catch the end of the service. Come on." She led them to a seat, not in the back out of the way—of course not—but darn near the first row of seats. At least they were at a point in the service where everyone was standing, so they were a little less noticeable. Rebecca parked the wheelchair at the end of a row and slid quietly in past Gigi. Fig snuck in behind her, between Gigi and Rebecca, who was thrusting an open prayer book into his hands and already singing along to a vaguely familiar melody as the rabbi, lifting the Torah into his arms, began parading down the center aisle toward the back of the congregation. As he passed, the people seated near the ends of each row reached out and touched the passing Torah scroll gently with their prayer books, and then brought the prayer books to their lips for a kiss. At the end of a row across the center aisle, Fig saw Jacob from his bar mitzvah class, looking sleepy as usual. When their eyes met, Jacob smiled slightly and gave Fig the peace sign. Fig smiled back.

As the rabbi turned the corner at the back of the group and headed down the outside aisle toward them, Rebecca turned in that direction and continued singing. Fig gazed at her for a moment. He enjoyed watching her sing, and her voice was lovely. When she noticed him looking at her, Rebecca smiled, her dark-grey eyes—they really were grey—sparkling. He smiled back, then looked down. He closed his eyes for a moment and let out a quiet sigh. Feeling the girl's arm brush against his, Fig opened his eyes just in time to see Rebecca and Gigi touch their prayer books to the Torah scroll in the rabbi's arms. Gigi brought hers to her lips, then extended it to Fig. He was surprised at how natural it felt to place a kiss upon the cover of this book, which had itself just kissed the Torah scroll.

He turned and smiled at Gigi, who was smiling up at him. It had been a bit more of an adventure than they'd bargained for, but they had done it. They were here.

SIXTEEN

The next morning, when Gigi stooped to sit on the sofa with the newspaper, the ball joint in her left hip snapped clean off. Fig was at Tony's, interviewing teammates for his soccer team documentary when his father called from the hospital. His dad had gotten home around 9:30 on Saturday evening and had allowed Fig to spend the night at Tony's with a few other guys from the team.

"I'm not going to be able to get away for a while," his dad said, after telling Fig about Gigi's new injury. "I want to wait until Gigi gets settled into a room here. I've talked to Mrs. Carr, and she's fine with having you hang out there till I can get you this afternoon."

"I need to be with Gigi," Fig said.

"I'll come get you as soon as they get her settled."

"I'll get Mr. Carr to drive me," Fig insisted.

"Listen to me, Fig," his father said. "Gigi's going to be fine. Once she's settled into a room, if she's feeling up to visitors, I'll bring you right down."

"I'm not a visitor," Fig said, irritated. His father wasn't

getting it. "I'm coming down now whether you like it or not, all right?"

There was a pause on the line.

"Do you need me to stop at the house and get anything?" he said, his voice slightly softer but still firm.

Another pause. Was his father really annoyed at him?

"Sure," he said, finally. "Actually, in the rush this morning, I forgot to take my stomach pills, and being in the ER is not helping any. Do you think you can get Mr. Carr to drive by the house on the way down?"

"No problem, Dad," Fig said, glad to be able to do something useful. It turned out the Carrs couldn't give him a ride, but Simmy's older brother agreed to do it, and within an hour Fig had found his way to Gigi's room.

She looked weak, tiny, very fragile. Seeing her huddled there on the hospital bed, her face turned away from him to expose the wrinkles on her neck, two images popped into Fig's mind in quick succession: Yoda from *Star Wars*, and a beautiful butterfly with a broken wing. "How is she?" he whispered, handing his father the medicine bottle he'd requested.

Gigi stirred. "Who's here?"

Fig moved to her, set his bag down on the floor, and took her small hand in both of his. "It's me, Gigi," he said. "Fig."

"Elijah, sweetie," she whispered, turning her head slightly toward him but not opening her eyes. "You came."

He gave his father a quick I-told-you-so glare. "Of

course I came," he said. He hated to see her looking so weak. "Are you in a lot of pain?" he asked.

Gigi shook her head slowly.

"They've got her on some pretty strong pain meds," Fig's father interjected. "That's why she's a little groggy."

At this Gigi opened her eyes for the first time and lifted her head slightly. "Not too groggy to know that you haven't had anything to eat all day, young man," she said, scolding her son-in-law. "Tell him you'll protect me while he goes to get something to eat," she instructed Fig. "He's been standing guard for hours now." Then she closed her eyes and put her head back down.

Fig and his father smiled at each other, and with a playful "Yes, ma'am," Fig's dad slipped out of the room.

Fig pulled up a chair to the side of the bed, and for a while he just sat holding Gigi's hand. Gigi seemed to doze a bit, but then after about fifteen minutes she opened her eyes.

"How did your interviews go?" she asked.

Gigi was amazing. "How do you even remember that's what I was doing with all you've been through this morning?" he asked.

Gigi just smiled.

"They're going okay," he said, answering her question. "Hey, want to see something pretty cool?" he asked.

"I'd love to," Gigi responded, her omnipresent smile weakened by pain and pain medication. "What do you have to show me?"

Fig perched his laptop carefully atop the sliding tray table in Gigi's room, and within moments Coach Lambert's face appeared on the screen. "It's the first scene from my documentary about the soccer team. I added music with Mr. Moffett after school Friday."

"Oh, Elijah, it's just marvelous," Gigi must have said a hundred times during the short clip. "Oh, I am very impressed. You've really got an eye for filmmaking, haven't you?"

"It's a big jump from 'The Adventures of Clay Man,'" Fig said, basking in the warmth of Gigi's response.

"I'll say it is," she said. "But save 'Clay Man.' It'll be fun to show off when you're a famous film director."

"I've still got a lot of work ahead on this one," he said. "But it's a heck of a lot more fun than just sitting around watching practice." Seeing that she had closed her eyes again, he hesitated to say what he wanted to say next.

"What are you thinking?" Gigi asked.

Now she was a mind reader? "How do you know I'm thinking anything?" he asked. "Maybe my mind is a total blank."

"I know you, Elijah Samuel," Gigi said. "Your mind is never a total blank."

He laughed. "I guess not," he admitted. "All right, fine. I've got an idea. For a *second* documentary."

"That's great," Gigi said. "It'll be good to have another plan in the works when you finish this one. I'm sure you'll get a lot more ideas as you go."

Looking at Gigi's wafer-thin form melting down into the hospital bed, he said solemnly, "I don't think I should wait on this one, though. I think I should get started soon."

"Well, you've certainly piqued my interest, young man," Gigi said, looking him earnestly in the eye. "All right, spit it out. Let's hear this urgent idea."

Fig wrung his hands together, blew into them. It was chilly in this room. He cracked his knuckles. "I'd like to make a documentary about my mother."

Gigi's eyes widened slightly, but she said nothing.

Now that he'd spilled it out there, Fig began to speak more quickly. "I've been doing some sketches. Remember the Ken Burns episode about the early years of baseball? He couldn't interview those early players because they were already gone, so he used a lot of still photos, letters and newspaper accounts, and interviews of people who remembered them. I've got a list of people I'd like to interview. People who remember Nina. Because I can't, really. Not much, anyway." He stared intently at Gigi, willing her to like the idea. "This documentary could be a way to help me remember."

Gigi couldn't sit up, but her head was fully off the bed and she was gazing at Fig with large, warm eyes. "It's just a lovely idea, dear," Gigi said. "I think you should do it."

Fig reached into his bag for his camera. "You're at the top of the list to interview," he announced. "Do you think we could get started today?"

Up till now, Gigi had only moved her head, but the prospect of being filmed in her current state was enough to motivate her to move her free hand as well. Covering her face, she said, "Not on your life. Not in here. Turn that camera off right now!"

In the aftermath of the broken hip, Aunt Simcha, who had been calling nightly to check on Gigi's progress and to grill Fig's father about her medical care, came to stay for a while to supervise her mother's care. In Hebrew, "simcha" means "joy," but as far as Fig could tell, it had been a long time since his aunt had lived up to the name. "Was Aunt Simcha ever happy?" he asked Gigi over breakfast on the Sunday morning in March when his father was headed to the airport to collect his sister-in-law. His dad would have scolded Fig for asking such an inappropriate question, but Gigi just laughed out loud.

"Oh, my, Elijah, sweetie," she said. "You're onto something there." Then she laughed aloud again, stopping with a grimace. "You can't make me laugh—it hurts too much."

"I'm not joking," Fig explained. "I'm serious. She never seems happy."

"I know, honey," Gigi said. "And I'm not laughing because it's funny. You just took me by surprise, that's all." She paused, biting her upper lip while she considered Fig's question. "Simcha was always a very serious child, but I don't think that means she was unhappy. She was happy when she married Alvin. She was very happy when her children were born. Don't let her get to you. She's just got her way, that's all."

Simcha's "way" was to take charge of whatever situation she found herself in, even—Fig soon learned—if it was someone else's home. From the moment she walked in the door, Aunt Simcha did not hesitate to bark orders at Fig or even at his father when she saw something that needed doing. For example, on the Monday morning after she arrived, she announced to Fig, "Dinner's at 6:30!" Racing out the door to school, he grunted, "Okay," and didn't think any more about it, so he was surprised when he and his dad walked in the door at 6:50 and his aunt shouted from Gigi's room, "I was wondering when you two were going to decide to waltz in—dinner's getting cold."

Every night, after she got things "whipped into shape," Fig could hear her call home to Charleston to make sure that proper order was being maintained in her absence. The night before Uncle Alvin and the kids were due to arrive for Passover, Fig overheard Aunt Simcha try to convince his father to have a nurse come to stay full time or even move Gigi to a nursing facility.

"Even teens need their mother home," she said, as if Fig's father had never considered the concept before. "I've missed most of Deborah's basketball season, and Shoshi's got softball and prom, graduation—I can't keep missing all that stuff."

"Go back home, Simcha," Dad urged. "We're doing fine here."

"You boys have busy lives," Aunt Simcha said. "You can't be here to give her the care she needs. Not the way things are headed."

What did grouchy old Aunt Simcha know, anyway?

Fig shut his bedroom door and pulled out his sketch-book. Without taking time to set up frames, he drew a picture of his uncle sitting on a couch, feet up on the coffee table, NASCAR cap on his head, a pile of TV dinners on the kitchen counter in the background. Under the sketch Fig penciled in a caption: "Yes, dear." He didn't know Uncle Alvin all that well, but he was pretty sure he would not show him the drawing.

SEVENTEEN

Soccer had moved back outside by the time Fig was cleared to participate in practice again. As he and his Dad were leaving the doctor's office, Fig got a text from a number he didn't recognize.

"All clear?" was all it said.

"Yeah, who's this?" Fig texted back.

"Coach Green," came the reply.

Then, "The Elites need a forward. Practice starts at 6:45."

And finally, "Coach Lambert knows."

Fig practically jumped for joy.

But he wasn't so thrilled when he didn't play at all in the Elites' first match after he joined the team, nor during the entire first half of the *second* match. Coach simply wasn't putting him in, which was frustrating, because Fig had been working hard. He felt good. No pain. He was ready to play.

The game was close, with each side scoring a single goal in the first half. Gus Starks even got the assist. Gus was still a bit of a ball hog, still barked out orders to his teammates, but Fig had to admit that his old nemesis had matured quite a bit since the fall, not only in terms of his own skills but also as a team player.

Late in the second half, match still tied, Coach Green finally sent Fig in to play up on the right side. Fig was surprisingly relaxed. He wasn't worried about impressing anyone. A couple of weeks of practice had convinced him that while his own foot skills had improved, his shoulder wasn't quite ready for banging bodies inside just yet. He just cruised the perimeter and stayed focused on finding an open man who could give his team a chance to score.

Fig made a few good passes to open teammates, but the opposing defense was tough, and for a while it seemed that the match might end up in a draw. Then suddenly, out of the corner of his eye, he spotted Gus with a clear line to the goal. Gus didn't make a big show of being open, didn't shout for the ball, but the two boys made eye contact, and Fig knew that he had a play. He directed a sharp pass to an open spot about eight yards out, and Gus sprinted in, striking the ball in mid-stride and burying it in the upper left corner of the goal. It was a perfect shot, impossible to defend.

Gus came running over. "Awesome feed, man! Right on the money!" In his enthusiasm, Gus pounded Fig on the arm. Gus's celebratory pounding sent searing pain shooting through Fig's shoulder, but the acknowledgement felt good.

"Thanks, man," Fig said, offering Gus a fist bump. "Great shot."

Coach Green asked the referee for a substitution and motioned for Fig to come off the field. He'd been in for less than five minutes, but that was a start.

REMEMBERING NINA
Interview with Elijah Samuel Newton

My, Elijah, you're even better looking in person than I'd imagined from the way the ladies talk about you.

Why, thank you, Fig. You're a bit of a hunk yourself.

Happy Birthday, by the way.

Thanks. Same to you.

Please state your full name.

Elijah Samuel Newton.

What is your relationship to Nina?

She's my mother, you idiot. Perhaps you should call her "Mrs. Nussbaum." Respect, you know.

Wouldn't that be Dr. Nussbaum?

Yes, I suppose so. Anyway, please continue.

So, bar mitzvah's only two days away, huh? Nervous?

Not as nervous as I was for the bris.

That's a good one.

Thank you. Anyway, I'm ready. I've been working hard, and I've had a good teacher.

Dr. Bischoff?

No, you fool. My grandmother. She coached me through the Hebrew, but more importantly, she helped me to understand why all this matters.

I know you're concerned about Gigi's health. What do you think? Will she be able to make it to the synagogue?

Not sure, Fig. But—and I'm sure this will sound corny to you—but I know that whether or not she's there in body, she'll be with me in spirit. In my heart. And my mother will, too. And, you know what else? They'll both be proud as peacocks.

You're right. That is corny.

Whatever.

EIGHTEEN

"What is that man doing on our seder table!" Aunt
Simcha's words—less a question than an outburst—had no
trouble making their way to Gigi's bedroom, where Fig was
reviewing table arrangements with Gigi.

"You don't recognize Hammerin' Hank?" he shouted
out to the dining room.

"Cameron who?"

"*Hammerin'* Hank. Hank Aaron," Fig said patiently, now
leaning against the doorpost of Gigi's room. "Greatest
home run hitter of all time. He broke Babe Ruth's all-time
home run record in the fourth game of the 1974 season."

If Aunt Simcha had any recollection of having skipped
out on the chance to witness this moment in sports history,
she certainly wasn't showing it. "What in the world is a
baseball player doing on our seder table?" she demanded.

Fig looked slyly at Gigi. He would have winked if he
was able. He'd have to practice that. "Oh, we always have a
photo of Hank Aaron on our seder table," he said. "I guess
you could say it's ... tradition."

Aunt Simcha rolled her eyes for the hundredth time of the day and marched back into the kitchen, from which, despite her foul mood, she was causing the most delightful aroma to emerge.

Fig returned to Gigi's bedside and held up his phone for her to inspect the table. Gigi hated not being able to do the cooking, but she was determined that being stuck in bed wasn't going to keep her from doing her part. "Elijah and I will set the table," Gigi had announced decisively the night before, when she and Aunt Simcha were reviewing the menu for the first-night seder.

Using his phone was Fig's idea. Gigi gave him instructions—which tables to move together, where to find the glass seder plate her great-grandmother had been given as a wedding present in Germany, knives to the right of each plate, cutting edge in—then Fig did what she asked and quickly scanned the table with his phone and took it to Gigi for the next instruction. Every once in a while he'd sneak some footage of Simcha in the kitchen or one of the cousins reading on the couch or tossing a football in the yard with Uncle Alvin, who was staying out of harm's way.

"Here's the Hank Aaron photo," said Fig, pointing. "I thought he could sit at Elijah's place for tonight—the real Elijah, I mean."

Gigi chuckled. Then she said, "The table looks beautiful, Elijah, sweetie. Now we need place cards. Do you think you can make up something nice on that computer of yours?"

"Sure," Fig said. "But I still don't understand why we've

got fourteen places. Me, you, Dad," Fig called out, ticking off the names on his fingers. "Aunt Jean's family is four, so that's seven. Aunt Simcha, Uncle Alvin, three kids, and an extra seat for Elijah. Who's number fourteen?"

"I invited Nadia Kaminsky," Gigi explained, a mischievous look on her face.

"Nadia who?"

"Kaminsky," Gigi repeated. "I think you know her, Elijah."

Fig's heart stopped. "Mrs. K.?"

Gigi nodded, smiling.

"You invited my science teacher? To our house?" Fig was in shock. Gigi simply nodded and smiled.

"For Passover?" The trauma of having his science teacher at his dining room table was hard to imagine. Grasping at straws, he asked, "Is she even Jewish?"

"She is, dear," Gigi assured him. "She is Jewish. And bright. And very kind." She paused. "And she is alone."

"Does Dad know about this?"

Like the villain in an old black-and-white movie, Gigi actually rubbed her hands together, savoring the mischief she was up to. "Not yet," she said. "Won't it be fun?"

The seder was a nightmare. The effort of supervising the table setting had left Gigi ready for a nap, and Aunt

Simcha refused to wake her when it was time to start the seder.

"Can't we wait to get started, then?" he asked.

Fig's question was answered by Aunt Jean. "I'm sorry, Fig," she explained. "The twins are getting hungry and it's going to be a long night for them as it is. Your grandmother really does need her rest, and she can join us when she's ready."

His aunts, who had seen each other a total of about three times before, were now best friends. Bonus.

"Well, I say if we're gonna start, we need to wake her," Fig said. "She won't want to miss seder with the family." He couldn't bring himself to say "her *last* seder," but he was thinking it, and the thought was too much to bear.

"She needs her sleep, sweetie," Aunt Simcha said, placing her hand firmly on his shoulder. Her protective tone annoyed him, as if she knew better than he did what Gigi needed or wanted. They had been doing just fine taking care of Gigi before Aunt Simcha got here. Fig shrugged his aunt's hand away and said, "Whatever." Taking his seat directly across the table from Mrs. K., Fig forced a smile and waved. Fig and Mrs. Kaminsky were seated near one end of the table, with Gigi's empty spot at the end left chairless so her wheelchair could be easily pulled up when she was ready. Gigi had insisted on seating Fig's teacher, whom she called "my special guest," next to her. And, of course, she had seated Fig's father next to Mrs. K.

Gigi's absence gnawed at Fig as Uncle Alvin, who sat at

the head of the table, began the seder, and even the warmth among the guests and the delicious smell of Aunt Simcha's matzoh ball soup could not pull Fig out of his dark mood.

As the family took turns around the table reading sections of the retelling of the Jewish Exodus from bondage in Egypt, Fig found himself viewing the scene as if he were watching a movie. Fig had made sure to seat Leah, a freshman in high school and his closest cousin by age, directly to his right as a buffer between himself and the squirmy twins. At the head of the table, Uncle Alvin sat between his wife and his two eldest daughters. The empty seat for Elijah the prophet (and Hank Aaron!) sat between Fig's father and Shoshi.

Fig was surprised to see Uncle Alvin and Aunt Simcha holding hands. Aunt Simcha, who usually insisted on being in charge of everything, seemed so happy *not* to be running this show. She gazed at her husband as he led the service, and she seemed to melt into his care and into the comfort of this highly structured meal. He noticed that his Charleston cousins had grown into very beautiful young women. And—*creepy*—he noticed that his dad and Mrs. K. were smiling at each other like a pair of teenagers.

When it was time for the *ma nishtanah*, the Four Questions, traditionally read by the youngest child, Uncle Alvin turned to Fig and said, "Elijah, why don't you read the Four Questions in English, and Shoshi can read them in Hebrew."

"Fig's been studying hard this year, Alvin," his father

jumped in. "I'm pretty sure he can handle the Hebrew." Fig's face felt like someone had just covered it with an electric blanket.

"My apologies," Uncle Alvin said to Fig. "Let's hear it, then."

His heart thumping in his chest, Fig managed to hack his way through the nine lines of Hebrew with whispered help from Leah on only two words. When he finished, Uncle Alvin cheered, "Well done," and the entire Charleston contingent clapped enthusiastically.

Aunt Simcha looked at him as if she were noticing him for the very first time. "You really *have* been working hard, haven't you?" she said proudly.

Fig breathed a sigh of relief as Mrs. Kaminsky took over reading, but as the retelling of the Passover story continued, Gigi's absence from the table began once more to gnaw at him. It was so unfair. Gigi was one of the kindest people he knew. *The* kindest. Why did a good person like Gigi, or like his mom, get this awful disease, when all kinds of mean and selfish jerks ran around healthy and free to do what they wanted? It was his father's turn to read now. *Blah, blah, blah.* How could everyone just sit here without Gigi, going on as if everything was just fine?

A sound from behind Gigi's door pulled Fig out of his daydream, and he quietly excused himself to check on her. He knocked lightly, then slipped quickly into the room and shut the door behind him, relieved to have a break from the crowd.

"You read beautifully," said Gigi. "I knew you would."

"Thank you," Fig said, softly. "I'm sorry we started without you," he said. "I tried—"

Gigi raised a hand to cut him off. "Don't be foolish," she said. "I'm not sure I'm up to getting out of bed anyway."

"Are you okay?" he asked, taking a seat in the chair next to her bed, a chair in which he found himself spending more and more time with each passing week.

"My stomach's bothering me a bit, that's all," she said softly.

"Can I get you anything?"

"No, Elijah, sweetie, I'll be fine."

For the next few minutes they just sat together. Sat. And breathed. And listened.

There was a knock at the door, and Uncle Alvin poked his head in. "May we join you?"

Gigi waved him in, and Uncle Alvin nudged the door open and came into the room, Haggadah in one hand, wine glass in the other. One by one the entire family came in until there wasn't a spot left to sit or stand. The older cousins sat on the edge of Gigi's bed. Uncle Bob hoisted the twins atop Gigi's dressing table where they perched like two little princesses reviewing a royal ball. Fig's dad and Mrs. K. entered last and stood in the doorway. Then, as if it were perfectly normal to lead a seder standing up around a hospital bed, Uncle Alvin said, "Leah, I believe it's your turn to read. We're on page thirty-one."

It was a little weird to see fourteen people crammed into

Gigi's bedroom, but it was also kind of nice. And it was certainly a lot better than conducting the seder without her. For the first time in a very long while, Fig felt as though everything was going to be okay. He had no clue what would happen next month, or next week, or even tomorrow. He knew his grandmother was dying. He could say the word now. Dying. Just as they were getting closer than he had ever imagined they would. And he knew that, as much as she'd love to be there, she might not feel well enough to make it to services on the morning of his bar mitzvah. One thing this year had taught him was that you just never know. You just never know. But—for this moment—Fig felt that everything was happening exactly as it was supposed to.

It was a very peaceful feeling.

He saw Gigi looking all around the room, grinning. She looked over at Fig and caught his eye, and he couldn't help but grin right back.

Acknowledgements

I am deeply grateful to the following people for their support of *Echo Still*:

My parents, Jim and Diane Tibbitts, who gave me the confidence to believe that I could do anything I set my mind to, not only by saying it over and over as I was growing up, but also by believing it themselves.

For gentle criticism and early support: Jim Garrett, Elizabeth Warshawsky, Sara Kamkha, Andi Davidson, Wendy Wasman, Michele Krantz, Alex Green, Jacob Voyzey, Jonathan Suna, Stephanie Silverman, Terry Dubow, Cindy Evans, Michelle Cydalka, Liz Krantz, Joanne Friedman, Devra Adelstein, and Diane Lavin.

For technical and artistic support for the final push: Milan Aviles, Cathleen Schaad, Leah Caruso and Sabrina Spangler.

To Bruce and Sid Good, for believing in the book when few others did.

To the Sydney Taylor Manuscript Award Committee of the Association of Jewish Libraries. To Jamie Light,

Catriella Freedman, and Madelyn Travis, and everyone at PJ Our Way. To Jessica Cuthbert-Smith at JCS Publishing Services Ltd.

To Charles Daroff for excellent guidance.

To Michael Leventhal at Green Bean Books.

Finally, to Kittie, Sarah, and Daniel, for making it all matter.

TIM TIBBITTS graduated from Brown University with a degree in American Civilization and holds advanced degrees in both American Literature and Education. He lives with his family in Shaker Heights, Ohio. He is also the author of the older teen/adult novel *Playing Possum*, available on Amazon.

Tim is available for readings, workshops, and (in-person and virtual) book club meetings. Contact Tim via his website, www.timtibbittsauthor.com.